Don't Believe
Your Lying Eyes

DON'T BELIEVE YOUR LYING EYES

A Darryl Billups Mystery

BLAIR S. WALKER

BALLANTINE BOOKS

NEW YORK

A Ballantine Book
Published by The Ballantine Publishing Group

Copyright © 2002 by Blair S. Walker

www.ballantinebooks.com

Library of Congress Cataloging-in-Publication Data
Walker, Blair S.
Don't believe your lying eyes : a Darryl Billups mystery / Blair S. Walker.
p.   cm.
ISBN 0-345-44682-8
1. African American journalists—Fiction. 2. Baltimore (Md.)—Fiction. I. Title.
PS3573.A42516 D66 2002   2002019072
813'.54—dc21

Manufactured in the United States of America

First Edition: June 2002

10   9   8   7   6   5   4   3   2   1

This book is dedicated to anyone who's ever
agonized over a missing loved one.

ACKNOWLEDGMENTS

Dr. Joseph Pestarnek, thank you for explaining the intricacies of the Maryland Medical Examiner's Office.

To my editor, Anita Diggs: I'm indebted to you for believing in me and for being a funny, insightful touchstone.

To my wife, Felicia: I rarely tell you what your unwavering support and encouragement mean to me—more than you can possibly know.

Last, I would like to thank the Creator for the many blessings You have bestowed upon me.

Don't Believe
Your Lying Eyes

PART

LONG TIME NO SEE

Man's capacity for self-deception is immeasurably greater than that for deceiving others. Every sensible person will testify to this fact.

—MAHATMA GANDHI

CHAPTER 1

Baltimore, Maryland, August 2002

Trying not to be too obvious, Darryl Billups watched in horror as a tiny, brazen insect skittered across the dinner table of his future in-laws.

It first appeared as a caramel-colored dot beside a plastic pitcher filled with grape Kool-Aid, before vanishing under a glass margarine dish. Darryl blinked several times, wondering if his eyes were playing tricks on him.

A mad dash past the pepper shaker answered that question, followed by a hard left directly toward Darryl's plate, which was piled high with pigs' feet, collard greens, candied yams, and two steaming squares of corn bread.

Squinting at the fast-closing marauder, Darryl confirmed

his suspicions—it was a baby cockroach! Now it was close enough that Darryl could make out its itty-bitty antennae twirling excitedly, homing in on enough cholesterol to block the arteries of every man, woman, and child within a fifty-mile radius of Baltimore. Little bastard probably even has a tiny bottle of Tabasco sauce with it, Darryl thought disgustedly.

He'd been dreading this first meeting with his future in-laws for weeks. He had dreamed up every question Tyrus and Sharon Winslow could possibly lob his way and had carefully crafted a response for each.

Darryl had prepared for everything except for a kamikaze roach bearing down on his dinner with the determination of Sherman marching on Atlanta.

"Mo' pig feets, sweetie?"

Startled, Darryl looked up into the face of Sharon Winslow, a petite, lemon-colored woman with keen, birdlike features and a startling sunburst Afro shot through with strands of gray.

"I'm doing great, Mom," Darryl replied.

From its perch on a grease-stained green wall opposite Darryl a nappy headed, brown-skinned Jesus stared down benignly from black velvet, watching to see what would happen next.

Darryl brought his napkin to his mouth and coughed to stifle the gag reflex starting to gather force in the back of his throat. Then he smoothly brought the napkin down on the flame red tablecloth and snuffed out the cockroach.

Dear Abby, when you're meeting your in-laws for the first time and grind a cockroach into their dinner table, should you wave your prize aloft and high-five the other guests?

Crumpling his catch into a ball, Darryl slickly eased it under the table and let the soiled paper napkin flutter to the floor.

He'd only eaten two glazed doughnuts all day, the better to have a demon appetite for Mrs. Winslow's cooking and make a favorable first impression.

That plan had disintegrated the moment Darryl cracked the front door and got a whiff of pig knuckles simmering at 175 degrees. Hungry as hell outside the Winslows' house, Darryl had little interest in eating after crossing the threshold.

It had been four years since swine last crossed his lips, when he'd gotten pissed drunk with some other *Baltimore Herald* reporters and scarfed down a slice of pepperoni pizza before realizing what he'd done.

Darryl had been pork-free since twenty-five, the age when he decided his body would benefit from less red meat. Pork was penciled off the menu instead of beef because Darryl was way too fond of his porterhouse steaks, London broil, and hamburgers.

Back in the days when he did eat pork, it was generally bacon and a smattering of ham every now and then. But not chitterlings and never, ever pigs' feet!

One of the more distasteful memories from his childhood was the pig-poop aroma of chitterlings bubbling on the stove. The other was going to his grandparents' farm in southern Maryland and watching pigs contentedly slosh about in their own smelly waste.

So today's main course had come as an unpleasant surprise. The cockroach sighting had merely served as an exclamation point.

Darryl glanced around to see if anyone else at the table had observed his actions.

Certainly not mildly inebriated Tyrus Winslow, a stocky, handsome man who was happily slurring the punch line to the twentieth cornball joke Darryl had heard since entering Mr. Winslow's East Baltimore row house.

Not Sharon Winslow, who was busily fishing something from between her front teeth with a burgundy fingernail.

Not Darryl's bourgeois sister, Camille, staring with obvious distaste at a set of faded gold curtains framing the dining room window in the Winslows' low-income dwelling. With down-turned lips she had disapprovingly taken in every minute detail of the Winslows' cheaply furnished home.

Her haughty, condescending air embarrassed and enraged Darryl. He wouldn't have invited Camille in a million years—that well-intentioned mistake was made by Darryl's fiancée, Yolanda Winslow, who apparently had witnessed the roach encounter. Poking dejectedly at her candied yams, Yolanda avoided Darryl's gaze.

"Anybody want sumpthin' outta the kitchen?" asked Mrs. Winslow, looking coldly at Camille. Proud and hypersensitive, Mrs. Winslow could sense Camille's disapproving air. And she didn't care for it one damn bit.

"You know, girlfriend," Camille said, sounding characteristically clipped and nasal, "I would love some more of that Kool-Aid. That stuff is the bomb!"

If prizes were given for sounding like a white suburbanite trying to talk black, Camille would be the undisputed champ.

Darryl cut his eyes at his younger sister. *Do you always have to be such a class-conscious jerk?* Hopefully, this evening from hell would be shutting down soon.

"They don't be sellin' Kool-Aid where you live?" Mrs. Winslow replied icily.

"Momma!"

Now Yolanda was the one shooting disapproving glances.

"Shit, baby, I keeps it real," Mrs. Winslow said tartly, raising her voice. "I ain't puttin' on no goddamned airs. I'll feed a stranger off the friggin' street, long as they don't act like they too good." Spoken to Yolanda but meant for Camille, who looked like she was headed to a society ball with her showy pearl broach and ostentatious green silk blouse.

Darryl kicked his sister under the table and vigorously shook his head. Camille had been zinging the Winslows all evening about their ramshackle house, their impoverished neighborhood, even their speech. The gibes were growing bolder and meaner by the minute, as though Camille was intentionally out to sabotage the evening.

Instead of heeding Darryl's nudge, Camille seemed emboldened by it. Looking in the general direction of Sharon Winslow, she began waggling her finger.

"Excuse me, sister girl," Camille said, sounding stilted with her ultraperfect diction. "But I happen to live in the city with soul folks, just like you do."

"Camille, let's call it a night," Darryl said quietly. "You need to apologize to Mrs. Winslow and we need to leave." Underscoring the seriousness of his words, Darryl pushed his chair back and stood up. It was time to get while the getting was good. Plus this would give him a reason not to touch the loathsome pork Mrs. Winslow had plopped onto his plate.

"Boy, you I like," Mrs. Winslow said, smiling warmly. "You good peoples, down-to-earth." The piece of collard greens she had been trying to dislodge from between her incisors was still firmly wedged there.

"I was giving you a compliment," Camille said unconvincingly. Mrs. Winslow ignored her and continued to smile at Darryl.

"Even though it was a bit much to serve Kool-Aid at a formal dinner," Camille muttered.

With surprising swiftness Mrs. Winslow leapt to her feet and flitted around to the same side of the table as Camille, who also got up, towering a good four inches over Mrs. Winslow.

"Bitch, I think you oughta git to steppin', like your brother said," Mrs. Winslow said darkly. The time for polite conversation and quaint social niceties had passed. Darryl grabbed Camille's arm.

A glowering Yolanda moved between her mother and prospective sister-in-law and gently pushed them apart.

Putting her hands on her hips, Camille stared down at

Sharon Winslow. "I just know you did not just call me *bitch*, you straight-from-the-ghetto—"

Swack! Displaying the hand speed of a youthful Cassius Clay, Mrs. Winslow deftly slapped the taste out of Camille's mouth with a forehand and struck her again with a backhand, ripping a button off Camille's expensive blouse in the process.

Camille stared in disbelief for a fraction of a second before viciously pushing her adversary back into the dinner table, sending pigs' feet, yams and grape Kool-Aid crashing to the floor with a horrible din.

Yolanda never made a sound, never shouted, never uttered a curse word. She simply made a fist and struck Camille in the stomach with such ferocity that Camille, Darryl, and Mr. Winslow all grunted in unison. Camille sank slowly to her knees, touching the carpet with her exquisitely coiffed, tastefully tinted brunette hair as she gasped for air.

All this was lost on Mrs. Winslow, who had scampered up from the carpeted floor and bounded into the kitchen. She popped out, waving a wicked-looking serrated steak knife over her head.

" 'Bout to put an East Baltimore ass-whipping on your bourgie ass!" Mrs. Winslow shrieked before her husband and Yolanda managed to overpower her and yank the knife away.

Darryl instinctively half crouched in front of his defenseless sibling. She may be a horse's ass, but she was one from the Billups stable. When push comes to shove and serrated steak knives start materializing, blood sticks with blood.

"G'wan outta here!" Mr. Winslow growled, easily restraining his tiny, profanity-spewing spouse, who barely rose to his shoulder. Mr. Winslow's jolly, semi-drunk demeanor had disappeared. Darryl guessed a deep bleeding cut on Mr. Winslow's left hand between his thumb and forefinger probably had something to do with that.

"Hurry up and git now, gawddammit!"

"I think you better do like he say," Yolanda said, shocked to the point of lapsing into Ebonics.

Grabbing Camille by one of her thickly muscled arms, Darryl pulled his sister to her feet. He mouthed "I'm sorry" to his fiancée, who didn't respond.

"Don't bring that stuck-up bitch up in here agin," Mrs. Winslow ordered as Darryl guided a wobbly Camille out the front door. The odds of Louis Farrakhan marrying Julia Roberts were probably better than those of Camille ever returning to the Winslows'.

Once out of the house and safely on the sidewalk, Camille immediately doubled over and began to greedily fill her lungs with air. Darryl watched unsympathetically, precisely because he suspected the entire display was a play for sympathy. No two ways about it, his sister's behavior had been inexcusable.

Several of the Winslows' neighbors watched from the marble front steps of their row houses, staring coldly at the high-society buppie who apparently had been shocked into speechlessness by the gritty sights, sounds, and smells of the inner city.

The fat cream-colored pearls on Camille's broach bobbed conspicuously as she panted like a winded dog. The pearls, along with the sparkle of Camille's diamond-encrusted tennis bracelet and the incessant twinkling of the fat two-carat diamond "friendship" ring she'd given herself, made Darryl nervous. He could handle his business but knew Camille was a bourgeois fish out of water in the 'hood. Plus it's hard as hell to throw down while wearing three-hundred-dollar black-leather Italian-made pumps!

Why had Camille even come to the Winslows'? To be nosy, of course! That was the only reason she'd accepted Yolanda's naive invitation and crashed what should have been an occasion to be cherished by Darryl, his fiancée, and the Winslows.

Darryl warily monitored a group of teenage boys nudging

one another and openly salivating at the sight of Camille's expensive jewels. She and her materialistic friends constantly strove to see who could acquire the showiest possessions, the wealthiest significant other, the most exotic vacation. All of them dropped names with such numbing regularity, it was a wonder their toes weren't swollen. One of their favorite pastimes was assembling to compare notes, then looking down their broad, buppie noses at anyone "struggling" along on less than six figures a year.

However, Camille's law degree, her partnership at one of Baltimore's top law firms, and her tales of Tahiti's "awe-inspiring, unspoiled idyll" hadn't prevented her from getting jacked by a woman twenty years older and fifty pounds lighter.

"You okay?" Darryl asked sharply. More faces were appearing in doorways and windows to take in the spectacle, drawn by Mrs. Winslow's scalding, high-decibel tirade, which could be heard clearly through her locked front door. Not eager to have her slice Camille into giblets and not thrilled to be in the company of a walking, talking Tiffany's display, Darryl began nudging Camille toward his black Japanese sports coupe. He was mad enough to whip Camille's ass on the sidewalk himself. She'd made what should have been a beautiful, memorable day ugly and forgettable with her boundless talent for rubbing people the wrong way. Truth be told, he was kind of glad the Winslow women had administered a tag team beatdown to his sister. It had been long overdue.

Darryl didn't utter a single word during the ride to his sister's luxury downtown high-rise on Charles Street and even left the radio off to underscore his silence. It was hard to believe he and Camille had both been raised by parents who stressed the importance of being polite and civil to people.

Camille was also quiet as Darryl's car passed through rough

urban neighborhoods that may as well have been the far side of the moon, given her unfamiliarity with them. But by the time they reached the third stoplight, the feisty trial attorney in her was starting to reemerge.

"Just because Yolanda has ignorant ghetto parents that's my fault, right?"

Darryl refused to dignify that comment. He was so angry that anything he said to Camille right now would only be regretted later.

Camille kept her big mouth shut a few more blocks before taking another stab at conversation.

"My main reason for coming was to give you moral support," she said quietly, hoping Darryl would turn and make eye contact.

Instead he continued to drive, concentrating on traffic as though deaf. Everything Camille had ever done in her entire life was driven by self-interest, so whom was she trying to fool?

"I saw how you dealt with that nasty roach," Camille said quietly. "Nobody was sure what to do, but I knew my big brother would come to the rescue."

I guess this is where I'm supposed to turn and smile and forget about what a total jackass you were? Nope, don't think so!

Looking at Camille out of the corner of his eye, Darryl saw the red outline of Mrs. Winslow's hand branded into Camille's cheek. A tiny trickle of blood oozed from her lower lip. Must have been one helluva slap.

Keeping his eyes on the road, Darryl opened his glove compartment and fumbled around until he felt a tissue. He handed it to Camille without comment.

"Thank you."

Camille dabbed at her lip and snorted angrily at the sight of blood.

"Okay, you really want to know what's up, Darryl? I may be speaking out of school, but I don't think Yolanda's good enough for you. That's how I really feel and I hope you don't take it the wrong way."

Was Darryl supposed to be flattered by that? It was typically arrogant of Camille to impose her judgment on the most critical decision of his life.

"Who in the hell do you think you are?" Darryl blurted, pulling in front of her high-rise condo building. "I decide who's 'good enough' for me, not you. Get out!"

"Mama feels the same way, Darryl. We both think you deserve better."

Really? Darryl's jaw twitched, but he said nothing. Mama was getting a call as soon as he got home.

"I'll call you later, okay?"

Darryl made eye contact with his sibling for the first time. Outwardly she was an attractive woman, but that was offset by the petty, materialistic troll living within.

"Why? We don't have a goddamned thing to talk about."

As soon as the door closed with a tinny clank, Darryl's foot was on the accelerator. He didn't even glance at his rearview mirror as Camille entered the lobby of her luxury condo complex.

It stung Darryl to think that his mother might actually disapprove of Yolanda. He'd never seen any indication of that—probably just one of Camille's hurtful mind games. Darryl pursed his lips. Mama didn't really think poorly of Yolanda, did she? Their arrangement as live-in lovers hadn't gone over well with Mama, but she and Yolanda seemed to get along beautifully.

Plus Mama treated Yolanda's young son, Jamal, like a little prince. Like a grandson.

No, Camille was the one with the superiority complex!

Darryl turned his radio to Morgan State University's station,

WEAA-FM. He felt dejected about the Winslows and knew he was probably being talked about like a dog. He guessed Yolanda would stick up for him, but he couldn't know for certain.

Darryl exhaled slowly, puffing out his freshly shaven cheeks. It annoyed him to have to apologize for the behavior of others. But Camille left him no choice. In a couple of hours, when emotions had cooled, he'd break out an olive branch and some knee pads.

Or maybe he should call sooner, in case Mr. Winslow had gone to the emergency room for that nasty-looking cut on his hand. *Damn you, Camille!*

Darryl felt badly about the way the evening had gone, particularly when his thoughts turned to Yolanda and what she must be enduring.

But Darryl was also feeling twinges of elation and relief, unleashing scalding guilt onto his conscience. In her ham-handed way, Camille had stumbled on Darryl's main misgiving about his relationship with Yolanda.

Unlike Camille, he didn't view himself as better than Yolanda. Just different. Whereas he grooved to the tranquil Brazilian jazz of Dori Caymmi, she vibed to the raw soul of Mary J. Blige. A 401(k) was his key to financial security—she put her faith in weekly Power Ball purchases. Roman Catholic versus Baptist; Bermuda versus Atlantic City; bachelor of science in journalism versus GED; History Channel versus the WB network.

Thankfully, their mutual respect, admiration, and love made their differences irrelevant most of the time. Sometimes, though, there were times Darryl wished Yolanda would be more . . . *ladylike* was the best way to describe it. Beautiful as she was, she had a habit of talking and laughing loudly in public that left Darryl mortified.

And every now and then she would unleash an "I ain't

got" and "he be having" that set Darryl's teeth on edge. He generally wouldn't say anything and couldn't put his finger on why it annoyed him so much. It just did.

Maybe the whole thing really was at age thirty-four Darryl still wasn't really ready for marriage. Sometimes he would single that out as the underlying reason for his occasional cold feet. Other times incompatibility got the nod. Sometimes it was a combination of the two.

Whatever the reason, the blowup at the Winslows' left Darryl feeling free and unencumbered. Because he'd subconsciously been seeking an escape clause in his relationship with Yolanda—just in case. Now he had one.

Darryl thought about that all the way to the modest two-story West Baltimore house he rented with Yolanda and Jamal. Jamal was at a baby-sitter's and Yolanda was probably still with her parents, leaving Darryl the rare luxury of an empty house.

Kicking off his shoes, he poured himself a glass of cheap Chardonnay and plopped down on the brown cloth sofa in the living room without bothering to turn on the stereo. Jamal's toys were put away and out of sight, allowing Darryl to look around and imagine that he was once again in a bachelor pad.

The wine went to his head quickly, sending a warm glow through his body and making him feel euphoric.

He rested his musty stocking feet on the coffee table, pleased not to hear Yolanda nagging him about it. Darryl drank slowly, savoring the wine and the peacefulness of a home where he could actually hear his thoughts.

That small pleasure alone seemed like an awful lot to sacrifice for matrimony.

CHAPTER 2

Grinning and humming an upbeat tune she made up as she went along, Adele Jones swayed rhythmically and lightly rubbed her hands together as she awaited the key to her treasure. In her mind's eye, she wasn't at a sprawling Safe&Sound self-storage facility on Reisterstown Road in West Baltimore.

No, Jones was an intrepid archaeologist about to uncover and catalog the undisturbed riches of King Tut's tomb. Surely the clerk inside Safe&Sound's office must know that—so why was Joe moving so slowly this August morning?

"Mornin', Miss Adele," he said in a painfully shy voice. Ever since he'd been a young boy, something about attractive women made conversation hard to come by. Especially a bronze-skinned beauty like Adele Jones, who had the power to vaporize his thoughts and sentences long before they reached his tongue.

She appeared to be fifty-eight or so, like he was, and had nary a wrinkle or crow's-foot on her smooth face. And good gawd, she had a way of making heavy-duty work gloves, frayed denim coveralls, and no makeup look good!

"That man called again, Miss Adele."

"He called a *second* time," Adele Jones tossed back her head, clearly delighted to have won the contents of Safe&Sound Unit 25 for a mere forty dollars. "Did he offer a thousand bucks again?"

"Naw. *Four* thousand."

Miss Adele beamed triumphantly. "Come on, Joe; find that key. I can't wait another second to find out what's in there!"

She had been boosted into bargain hunter's heaven because someone had carelessly missed two twenty-five-dollar monthly payments on Unit 25 after years of religiously mailing envelopes with Baltimore postmarks and no return address.

A string of 180 consecutive monthly payments had been snapped in June, and the July payment was missed also. Safe&Sound responded by allowing the contents of Unit 25 to be auctioned to Adele Jones for forty dollars. That was two days ago, the same day a desperate-sounding anonymous man offered to pay $1,000 in cash if the lease on Unit 25 could be reinstated.

After that proposal was turned down, the man called back the following day and offered to give Joe $4,000 in cash to put the lease on Unit 25 back in force. The mystery man sounded like someone used to giving orders and having them followed.

Joe would have given his eyeteeth to oblige. But as luck would have it, a visiting Safe&Sound executive happened to be in the office and was practically staring down Joe's throat.

At least Joe had been able to alert Adele Jones to the impending auction of Unit 25. Thanks to the tip, the antique-loving retired schoolteacher was the only bidder. She planned to keep one or two prized possessions for herself, then sell the rest of her self-storage booty to a local thrift store for a tidy profit.

So Adele Jones rocked impatiently on the balls of her feet as Joe pooted around the office like an old fogey, searching for the key to Unit 25. He finally found it and took pains to lightly brush his hand against Miss Adele's as he handed her the key.

Never acknowledging his touch, she pivoted on her finely proportioned hips and walked out the office door, moving rapidly in the direction of Unit 25's locked, blue corrugated metal door.

She was watched by a pair of admiring eyes until she disappeared from sight. "It's silly to get tongue-tied round that fine woman," Joe muttered to himself.

He was still daydreaming about Miss Adele when the primal sound of a screeching female voice rang out about thirty minutes later. Grunting, Joe dropped his pencil. Another scream sounded, the noise reverberating off the corrugated metal doors of dozens of storage units lined up in neat rows.

Scooping up a rusty ax he kept stashed under his desk, Joe sprinted out the office door and turned left, in the direction of Unit 25. Miss Adele was standing in front of the unit with her hands jammed to her mouth, terror-stricken.

Joe laughed nervously, partially out of relief that Adele Jones was okay and also because he guessed she'd seen a mouse. Them critters had an irritating habit of finding cracks in the concrete walls, then making nests inside folks' belongings and occasionally scaring the hell out of Safe&Sound customers.

"Exterminator comin' next week," Joe blurted, suddenly feeling sheepish. He'd been meaning to call the pest control folks for a month but had only gotten around to it the previous day.

He strode confidently toward Unit 25, ready to bludgeon

the offending vermin into oblivion. The wooden-handled ax felt reassuring in his thick right hand as Joe surveyed the contents of Unit 25. He couldn't talk to his damsel in distress worth a damn, but he could certainly get her attention with bold, heroic action.

Unit 25 had the typical attic/basement smell that was in most of the other Safe&Sound units on Reisterstown Road. It contained neatly stacked boxes, appliances, clothes, the usual flotsam and jetsam of a mundane existence placed on hold.

What distinguished Unit 25 from the other sixty-one self-storage modules was its time-capsule quality. It was like a museum dedicated to the 1980s; no one had disturbed its contents since dropping them off almost two decades ago.

An ultralight layer of dust coated everything, including an open shoe box containing four bottles of Dark & Lovely shampoo, a brush and comb filled with strands of long brown hair, and two circular containers of Royal Crown hair pomade.

There were a few pieces of classy-looking furniture, including a sofa decorated in flowery pastels and a simple love seat made with a dark wood of some kind. Whoever rented this unit sure loves music, Joe thought, gazing at eight cardboard boxes brimming with vinyl by Lionel Richie, Johnny Mathis, Smokey Robinson, and Earth Wind & Fire, among others.

In the meantime, Miss Adele stood sentry out front, her eyes continuing to yell a mute warning. When she started signaling for Joe to come back outside, he turned his back so she wouldn't see the smile spreading across his face. Instead, he began to make his way toward the rear of the cluttered storage unit.

Miss Adele had cleared a four-foot passageway through the middle of the fifteen-by-thirty-foot unit, opening boxes and looking things over as she progressed.

She had made it all the way to the back wall, where her path had taken her to a six-foot mahogany wardrobe sitting flush against the wall. Joe could see some of its contents strewn about and expected to find it filled with BB-sized mouse droppings. Chuckling under his breath, he lowered the ax to his side and made his way to the back of Unit 25, taking care not to bump into feminine-looking lamps, two mattresses bound together, a stack of 1984 *Ebony* and *Jet* magazines, and a white Westinghouse dryer that looked to be brand-new.

A light blue rag that appeared to be stained with burgundy paint was off to one side of the wardrobe. Closer examination showed that it was a ruffled blouse.

Two tan canvas tarpaulins had been strewn on the floor to the left of the wardrobe, apparently by Miss Adele.

Tiptoeing now, so as to catch the mouse off guard, Joe slowly unclasped the door of the wardrobe with his free left hand. He pulled it open in one fierce motion, hoping to surprise the rodent in its tracks.

But there was no mouse inside, only a rumpled mass of black roofing plastic.

"Hello, mister mouse!" Joe laughed as he yanked the tarp back. His smirk disappeared and the thunderclap yelp of a terrified adult male echoed throughout the corridors of the Safe&Sound. At the same time, a sickening smell reminiscent of vinegar and spoilt buttermilk rose like a howl to assault Joe's nostrils.

The roofing plastic fluttered from his fingers, sending a nimbus cloud of white lime dust billowing across the concrete floor of Unit 25. Feeling an uncomfortable tightness in his chest, Joe turned to leave Unit 25, his shoes seeming to float over the concrete floor instead of touching it.

He strolled out to Miss Adele, who was still clutching her pretty brown cheeks, and fainted at her feet.

CHAPTER 3

Across town from the Safe&Sound self-storage depot, inside a richly appointed oak-paneled office, with pastel highlights not usually associated with a male occupant, the developments of Unit 25 were quickly blossoming into a nightmare of unthinkable proportions.

"What do you mean, Unit Twenty-five was auctioned, Gregory?" the man in the oak-paneled office whispered frantically, leaning forward in an overstuffed beige leather chair whose color matched the walls. "Why did you leave it there in the first place? You've had *eighteen years* to deal with this problem. Mary Mother of Jesus!"

"I-I thought it would be cool in there," Gregory stammered.

The man in the oak-paneled office nervously ran a brown hand over his close-cropped wavy black hair. He smoothed it methodically, searching for the right words to express his astonishment and displeasure. *Incompetent asshole* sprang to mind, but that wasn't exactly what excitable Gregory needed to hear at the moment.

As he listened to Gregory's frantic-sounding breathing over the phone, the man in the oak-paneled office made himself a vow: He would never, ever allow this slipup to jeopardize who and what he had become. He'd traveled too far, worked too hard, and sacrificed too much—including his first marriage.

He'd struggled through Yale Law School twenty-five years ago, working three nights a week and devouring so much tuna and baked beans that the pungent aroma of tuna turned his stomach to this day. But it had all been worth it, because his Yale law degree had pried open doors that allowed him to become powerful and revered.

Now scores of people looked to him daily for guidance and he was able to reside in a hideous, pricey brown-and-white Tudor people thought was attractive because it was located in Roland Park, one of Baltimore's fanciest neighborhoods.

Not bad for someone who'd grown up as a numbers runner in the city's murderous Murphy Homes high-rise housing project.

The man in the oak-paneled office frolicked every week with a stunning, sexually insatiable mistress fifteen years his junior and had a preferred table at the Center Club, where the city's top businessmen preened over downtown power lunches served high over Baltimore's scenic Inner Harbor, fifteen stories below.

And now an unexpected variable was threatening to obliterate a neatly ordered existence assembled with mother wit, hard work, and a charisma most men could only dream of.

He was making a positive impact on too many lives to lose everything just because of what was locked inside Safe& Sound's Unit 25 on Reisterstown Road.

The man in the oak-paneled office loosened his two-hundred-dollar gold silk tie, grasped the sides of his desk, and forced himself to take in deep, slow breaths.

By the fourth breath, the panic threatening to run rough-shod over his brain was starting to die down. After three more breaths, a workable solution to his horrible predicament was beginning to materialize.

"Brother Greg, brother Greg," the man in the oak-paneled office said soothingly. "Ain't nothin' but a thang, man. All we need to do is chill, brother, just chill."

"But what if they find out—"

"Shhhhh! Don't talk a bunch of negative stuff to life, man. We don't need to be going through a whole bunch of unnecessary changes, because we haven't done a thing, Greg. Are you feeling me?"

"Yeah. Okay." The tone was hesitant, unconvinced.

"What happened to the Safe&Sound rent money, bro'? You playing the ponies at Pimlico?!" The man in the oak-paneled office had a smile in his voice, for he'd learned hu-mor is a great counterbalance to towering ambition, superior intelligence, and an unrelenting mean streak.

"Ain't no excuse, man. My bad—I blew it," Gregory said in a voice husky with shame. "I had the money; I just forgot."

"All right already. Let's move on." In less than ten seconds the fake warmth and friendliness had given way to cool cal-culation. "Greg, we need to stop talking over the phone, okay? Meet me at my place tonight. And, Greg—please come alone."

Gregory pulled his cell phone away from his ear and gen-tly folded it shut. He would show up alright—with his 9mm semiautomatic tucked in his waistband.

The man in the oak-paneled office might be his brother, but he still didn't trust him worth a damn.

CHAPTER 4

Hands welded to her hips, Yolanda Winslow glared down at Darryl Billups, whose stocking feet rested on the coffee table in their living room. A half-full glass of amber wine sat perilously close to his left foot. He had been snoring on the couch like a runaway freight train when Yolanda entered their home, still steaming over the incident at her parents' house.

"Don't patronize me, goddamn you, Darryl. I don't deserve to be treated like some idiot!"

Few things are as irritating as trying to fight a significant other who yawns noncommittally, refusing to rise to the bait. Yolanda had called Darryl's sister, Camille, everything but a child of God, and all he would do was nod mildly and shrug. And every time he did, Yolanda felt a mounting urge to take her fist and knock the crap out of Darryl, like she'd done with that heifer sister of his.

"Why in the fuckin' hell didn't you tell me that simple cow didn't have any manners? That ign'ant bitch!"

Fuckin' hell? Yolanda never could cuss worth a damn when she was really ticked. Darryl shrugged, the faintest hint of a smile flickering briefly across his handsome face. "Sweetie, you never asked."

Yolanda scowled furiously, her thick eyebrows nearly forming a single hairy line across her brow.

"Well, I'm asking you now!" she screamed. "Got any more shitheads in your family that I can't take to my parents' house? I know somethin' else, too—you need to wipe that smirk off your face. My father needed twelve stitches, so ain't nothin' funny up in here."

"Yolanda, tell you what. Stop screaming and cussing, or we can end this conversation. I already apologized for Camille and said I was sorry about your father. I'm sorry, okay? I didn't want things to turn out like they did. Is your pops okay?"

"If you gave a damn, you would have called. But you're only concerned about yourself, just like your selfish, slut-ass sister."

Darryl didn't look up into his fiancée's face. Instead he stared a hole into her kneecaps and silently counted.

"As a matter of fact," Yolanda continued, "if your mother had any common sense, she would have taught that heifer some manners a long time ago."

Muttering darkly, Darryl bounded from the couch and stalked past Yolanda, headed for their bedroom. Stopping in front of his dresser, Darryl yanked off his pants and slung them toward the window on the north side of the bedroom. The louvered shades shuddered violently before crashing to the bedroom floor.

If there was one thing Yolanda absolutely hated, it was clutter and disarray. Well, she'd get a little of it now.

And if there was one thing he absolutely hated, it was high-decibel cussing matches, fueled by emotion instead of logic, maturity, and mutual respect. Darryl had never forgotten how his parents used to verbally pound each other while he wrapped a pillow around his young ears and sang softly to block out the horrible noise. Even though he was a grown man now, the little boy inside still cringed at the sound of a man and woman going at each other.

If Yolanda was to be his wife, which was looking less and less likely, they would need to start discussing their differences calmly and sensibly.

Darryl slid out of his shirt next and hurled it into the closet, knocking down several wire coat hangers. That act took some of the edge off his anger but also made him feel childish and oafish.

Spying a gray Baltimore Ravens sweat suit on the bed, Darryl picked it up and slid it on. Without bothering to remove his black dress socks, he slipped his feet into a pair of white-and-black tennis shoes and tucked in the laces without tying them.

By now, Yolanda had moved to the bedroom door and taken on a confrontational pose in the doorway. That was in keeping with her modus operandi—always ready to sprinkle a few more gallons of kerosene on a raging fire.

Ignoring her, Darryl picked up the pants he'd hurled across the room and fished his car keys and wallet out of a lint-filled pocket. Then he casually dumped the pants in a disheveled heap in front of the dresser, for Yolanda's benefit, and began moving toward the bedroom door.

Yolanda didn't flinch as he approached. Only at the last conceivable second did she move aside, barely giving her fiancé enough room to exit and brushing against him lightly as she did.

Her touch was the last thing he wanted to feel.

"Grow up!" Darryl barked over his shoulder. "And you know I don't *play* that stuff about people's mamas."

"Like I give a shit!"

That's right; go ahead and kill every warm feeling I have, you simpleton!

Darryl slammed the front door hard enough to shatter its diamond-shaped glass window.

He sat in his car for fifteen minutes without bothering to start it, debating whether to call one of his old girlfriends who would welcome him with open and passionate arms, no questions asked. It was definitely a tempting proposition. But that would only be a temporary solution. The next day Darryl would still need to make some hard-nosed decisions about his and Yolanda's relationship. Tonight had marked the first time he'd ever thought about disrespecting Yolanda in that way. It was as though she sensed he was looking for an out and was trying to force his hand.

Yolanda's habit of nudging bad arguments toward physical confrontations unsettled Darryl. He had never touched a woman in anger in his life and didn't like being goaded. Why was she pushing to see if there was a dark, cowardly blemish on his heart? What was wrong with using words to solve differences?

Darryl's thoughts drifted to Camille and he grimaced. Camille had already come to the condescending conclusion that Yolanda was a "round-the-way" girl. At the moment, Darryl had to admit that appeared to be the case.

Fully aware that he'd feel sheepish and disgusted once his anger evaporated, Darryl turned the ignition key to his sports coupe. The engine caught smoothly on the first try.

Not sure where he was going either figuratively or literally, but knowing he had to get the hell away from Yolanda, Darryl jammed his car into first gear and gently let out the clutch.

As soon as he strolled into the bachelor pad of John "Mad Dawg" Murdoch, Darryl knew he'd made a mistake. Sure, Dawg would listen attentively, wouldn't be judgmental, and would dolefully shake his head and commiserate about the mysterious, ever-changing state of the female psyche. But in terms of being able to shed light on Darryl's dilemma, all Dawg had was a little candle.

That's because Dawg was pathologically incapable of sustaining a relationship longer than nine months, let alone one culminating in matrimony. Darryl often wondered if it was coincidence that Dawg couldn't stay in relationships longer than the time necessary for human gestation. Probably not.

Mad Dawg could wax eloquent about boy-meets-girl, boy-charms-girl, boy-seduces-girl. But his body of knowledge regarding boy-coexists-with-girl could fit on the head of a match.

Sitting in a lotus position on the floor, his red, beady eyes staring at Darryl through a fog of sweet marijuana smoke, Dawg wasn't the sounding board Darryl needed at the moment. Weighted down with adult problems, Darryl had come seeking answers in the smoke-filled sin den of a thirty-something man-child.

Dawg's black-and-orange dreadlocks bobbed in unison with a Cuban jazz CD playing so loudly that the massive wooden speakers to his stereo quivered and vibrated as they performed a jittery salsa.

For the first time since "Dinner at the Winslows'," Darryl smiled. He wondered if the other tenants in the apartment had given up on Mad Dawg. Either that or Dawg had driven everyone deaf.

The *Baltimore Herald*'s premier sports columnist wore a skimpy purple thong that allowed his narrow buns to touch the carpeted floor and caused Darryl to avert his eyes. Judging from lanky Mad Dawg's sunken, hairless chest, he'd never seen the inside of a gym, despite writing about muscle-bound jocks for a living.

A stunning, small-breasted black woman with short reddish hair reclined on the floor, her eyes blissfully closed as her head lay in Mad Dawg's lap. She wore a black bra and a white skirt that appeared to have been hastily donned just prior to Darryl's arrival. Her stockings were strewn across the top shelf of Mad Dawg's wall-mounted bookcase.

"Whazzup, boy?"

"No haps, Dawg." Darryl eyed the pretty redhead, who opened her eyes briefly, smiled warmly as though she and Darryl had been bosom buddies in some distant millennium, then blissfully drifted back into semiconsciousness. Even through she was obviously bombed out of her mind and hadn't uttered a single syllable, Darryl found her intriguing.

"Didn't mean to crash your spot while you were entertaining, man," he said, glancing at his watch. On a small table behind Dawg a red Lava lamp was busily erupting to the beat the band.

Dawg yawned and repositioned his long, bony legs by grasping the ashy soles of his ski-like feet. Darryl made a note not to shake Dawg's hand on the way out.

"Everything's good, man," Dawg said drowsily, motioning toward a spot opposite him. "Take a load off, kid."

Looking unconcerned, Dawg casually picked up a *Sports Illustrated* magazine off the floor beside him. A meticulously rolled blunt about the size of a Louisville Slugger popped into view. Dawg glanced at Darryl with half-closed eyes that almost seemed to be mocking before shifting his gaze back to the monstrous joint.

"G'wan, man; dig in. I can tell somethin's eating at you."

Darryl laughed, partially because Dawg possessed an uncanny funk detector for sniffing out Darryl's bad moods. And because Dawg knew perfectly well that for Darryl, smoking weed had gone the way of eating pork.

It was probably wise to leave now, given that he probably already smelled like a five-alarm fire thanks to all the smoke in the air. Yep, he should be moving toward the door and fishing out his car keys . . . yet Darryl made no effort to move.

Maybe it was the accommodating, free-spirit vibe in the air. Or more likely it was a subconscious passive/aggressive thing to get back at Yolanda by staying out late.

"Got a brew?"

Of the phrases most often used to describe Mad Dawg Murdoch, *gracious host* wasn't one of them. He twisted his head in the general direction of the kitchen, then reverently picked the unlit joint off the carpet. Dawg examined it slowly, much as a jeweler might admire an exquisite diamond, brought it to his lips, and lit a match.

That was Darryl's cue to leave the scene of the crime and rummage through the refrigerator for a cold one.

Even by pitiful bachelor-pad standards, the interior of Dawg's icebox was laughably disgusting. A malignant-smelling cool air mass flowed out the moment the door opened, forcing Darryl to hold his breath.

"Damn, Dawg! Ever hear of disinfectant, sleazebag? Or baking soda?" Darryl wondered why women didn't run screaming from a dwelling containing such an offensive refrigerator.

Sitting on the top shelf was a wilted grapefruit sporting a luxuriant growth of bluish-green mold. Until that moment, Darryl hadn't known that grapefruit rind contained the proper mixture of nutrients to support mold spores.

On the bottom shelf was a battered-looking open quart of milk with a June 22 expiration date. Darryl shuddered—today's date was August 3.

A disintegrating pastrami on rye sandwich was encased in

a plastic sandwich bag filled with mustard-colored ooze. Toward the back were two D-cell batteries, sitting on either side of a huge, vein-covered, brown dildo standing upright on a little platform. Gulping, Darryl decided that "don't ask, don't tell" was the best way to deal with that last item.

Finally spotting two brown bottles of beer—one half-empty, one full—amid the clutter, Darryl grabbed the fresh one and slammed the refrigerator shut. It took a good five minutes for its rancid odor to disappear, not that Dawg and his thoroughly fried guest paid any heed.

Hardly a neatnik himself, Darryl looked at Dawg oddly. Only two kinds of people could maintain a refrigerator so nasty—those who were incredibly trifling and those in dire need of immediate professional help. *Which are you, my brother?*

Guessing correctly that Dawg's carpet probably hadn't seen a vacuum in months, Darryl plopped down on a blue plastic inflatable chair that looked like it belonged in a teenage college student's dorm room.

Ordinarily not much of a drinker, tonight Darryl craved alcohol. The brew he plucked from Dawg's fridge tasted like nectar of the gods. Every malt, hop, and bubble of carbonation tickled Darryl's palate to perfection.

He guzzled contentedly, amusing himself by watching Dawg, whose dreadlocks made him look like a fire-breathing Methuselah. Sensing Darryl's eyes on him, Dawg turned. Grinning, he held his joint out to Darryl, who shook his head.

"I'm good, Dawg," Darryl murmured, taking another swig from his brew. Dawg extended the same offer two minutes later, and Darryl again waved him off with a laugh.

The third time was a charm—before Darryl realized what he was doing, he had reflexively grabbed the joint from Dawg's slim fingers. He chuckled and gently set his empty beer bottle on the floor.

"Satan, get your dreadlock-wearing ass behind me!" he said in a booming voice. For some reason, he and Dawg found this uproariously funny and fell out cackling. It had been aeons since they had had an old-fashioned meltdown, and by all appearances that's exactly where they were headed.

Frankly, Darryl needed to blow off some steam. Dawg, on one hand, seemed to have a built-in pressure-release mechanism when it came to handling tension and stress. Darryl, on the other hand, had a maddening way of clutching those two monsters to his bosom and marinating in their corrosive juices.

"Bring it full circle, bro," Dawg said, smirking. "Nothing to it but to do it!" Maybe it was Darryl's imagination, but there seemed to be a sneer in Dawg's voice, like he was talking to some nerd, instead of a charter member of the posse.

"Man, you think I'm scared?" Darryl said contemptuously. "This weak shit wouldn't get a fly high!"

Darryl put the glowing joint to his lips and took a deep drag, creating a red-tinged aura around him in the smoke-filled air. A cascade of burning hot volcanic ash flowed from the homemade cigarette and into Darryl's windpipe and lungs, turning his chest into a raging conflagration!

Darryl's body heaved spasmodically as cough after gut-wrenching cough left his body. He raised such a ruckus that it actually drowned out the high-decibel assault pouring from Dawg's stereo and jolted Dawg's slumbering guest into consciousness, her expression that of someone unexpectedly confronting Armageddon.

"Tried to warn you, boy!" Dawg cried, cackling. "Ain't nothin' weak in the Dawg pound, son. So don't come up in here half-steppin'."

Thoroughly embarrassed, Darryl tried to coax a snappy reply from his singed vocal cords. However, the best he could do was croak out a couple of wheezy hacks.

His lungs finally ended their noisy protest, enabling Darryl to notice just how novel and innovative Dawg's Cuban jazz was. Darryl didn't hear it so much as become one with it. He closed his eyes and felt the sensation of being suspended in midair, floating amid a sea of musical notes emerging from Dawg's stereo. The *thump-thump!* of the bass was in perfect harmony with each beat of Darryl's heart, while the electric guitar seemed in sync with the electrical impulses racing through his brain.

But as exceptional as the musicians were, the shining gem was the female vocalist accompanying them. Even though Darryl knew no Spanish beyond *adios*, he suddenly understood everything she was singing.

"Good shit, ain't it?" Dawg said, smirking. Happy that he'd coaxed Darryl to fall off the wagon, breaking an eight-year moratorium.

"You meant to do this, man, didn't you?" Darryl said darkly, cannabis-induced paranoia settling over him like a thundercloud.

Seeming to go stone sober in the bat of an eye, Dawg waved his hand dismissively. "Hey, man, you came over here to me crying the blues about Yolanda. You're a grown ass man—nobody can make you do nuthin' you don't want to do. Knowwhadumsayin'?"

Darryl grinned sheepishly, knowing he'd only sound foolish if he tried to counter that logic. The fog he was in had nothing to do with Dawg and everything to do with his desire not to think about Yolanda or their relationship. On that count, at least, he'd succeeded magnificently.

Darryl stretched out on the floor, taking pains to lock his fingers behind his head, lest his closely cropped black hair touch the dirty carpet.

"Wanna hit this again, boy?"

Darryl merely smiled and closed his eyes, continuing to glide through musical crescendos and percussion solos like a scuba diver floating languidly through a forest of swaying kelp.

When he opened his eyes, the stark, uncompromising rays of the morning sun slapped his retinas awake. Darryl was still reclined on the floor, the fabulous music was no longer playing, and Dawg and his lady friend were gone. Only the Lava lamp seemed intent on recapturing the spirit of the previous evening, furiously tossing out chunk after chunk of glowing red magma.

Darryl glanced at his watch and his stomach muscles tightened. It was a little after nine-thirty. What day was it? Darryl relaxed, remembering that it was Saturday—he didn't have to report to the *Baltimore Herald*.

Then Darryl remembered that he'd walked out on Yolanda the previous night and stayed out until morning. Now he had some explaining to do.

Enraged a few hours ago, he now felt embarrassed and contrite. Darryl rose slowly from the floor, feeling fuzzy-headed and off his game, which was one of the reasons he'd stopped puffing ganja in the first place. He hated not feeling sharp and in control.

He stretched, making his neck and right knee sound like popguns discharging. Darryl was too old to be smoking pot like some pimply-faced adolescent, then passing out on the floor. His sore, stiff back would attest to that.

No sense fretting over it now because the deed was done. So was the weed.

CHAPTER 5

Baltimore City homicide detective Scott Donatelli scowled as he surveyed the musty innards of Unit 25 at the Safe&Sound self-storage facility. Two civilians had already bumbled through the place like bulls frolicking through Pamplona, tainting and obliterating trace and physical evidence that had probably been pristine and undisturbed for years.

Donatelli didn't saunter into people's workplaces rearranging paperwork on their desks or screwing around with their computer files. So he always felt vaguely violated when confronting a badly contaminated homicide scene.

Especially the one inside Unit 25, because moldy oldies were Donatelli's favorites. Anybody could solve a murder committed twenty-five minutes earlier by some hot-blooded perp who lived within a ten-block radius of the murder scene. But cracking an old unsolved took special skill and dedication, in Donatelli's eyes.

One of the greatest things about his job was being able to knock on the door of some smug graying perp and collar him for a murder committed in the distant past.

Tall and sinewy, Donatelli stroked his shiny black goatee agitatedly as the sun glistened off a mane of jet-black hair that elicited disapproving glances from his superiors. Donatelli's better-than-average record at closing homicide cases was the reason his scraggly locks were grudgingly tolerated.

"Come on, come on. Let's get this show on the road," he muttered.

"Didja say something, Scott?" Detective Thelma Holmes asked. A big-boned black detective who'd been an Eastern District foot patrolwoman for six years, Holmes had been promoted to homicide three months earlier.

Frankly, Donatelli resented the hell out of her presence, because the art of ferreting out homicidal miscreants was only perfected through years of trial and error. He didn't have the time or inclination to play wet nurse to a newbie. Furthermore, Donatelli was certain Holmes was an affirmative action baby, because she'd been promoted to homicide in six years, versus his eight.

Donatelli was also highly suspicious of Holmes's flawless copper-colored skin, full, beautiful lips, and light brown eyes that glowed with a luminescence he had noticed on more than one occasion. Full-bodied Detective Holmes was too pretty to be a real cop—Donatelli would bet anything some male captain or major was fast-tracking her career in return for some after-hours target practice.

Truth be told, no one would ever come close to filling the shoes of his former partner, Phil Gardner. Donatelli had worshiped Gardner, a black detective who'd died from a perforated ulcer while working on the Confederate flag murder case two years earlier. A series of killings that had brought tremendous acclaim to *Baltimore Herald* journalist Darryl Billups, as though Donatelli had nothing to do with cracking the case.

"Detective, why are those witnesses talking to each other?" Donatelli snapped as he pointed to Safe&Sound manager Joseph Dennis and a customer, Adele Jones. "Witnesses need to be separated until they give statements, Detective Holmes. The reason for that—"

"Is so they won't be able to get their heads together and fabricate a story. Scott, I interviewed them already," Holmes shot back, pulling a narrow spiral notebook from the back pocket of her black slacks and flipping it open. "Besides, patrolmen keep witnesses separated, not detectives."

Replacing the notebook, she gazed levelly at Donatelli. Being the only black female on a homicide squad of more than fifty detectives meant some tongue-biting was in order, not exactly Thelma Holmes's strong suit. She would hold her fire for at least another month—after that, all bets were off.

If only Donatelli could move beyond the usual white-boy assumptions, Holmes thought, smiling faintly to mask her rising irritation. If he did some digging, he'd see that she'd graduated first in her 1996 police academy class, earned a chemistry degree cum laude from Morgan State University in Baltimore, and had a brown belt in tae kwon do and an exemplary record since joining the force.

She'd cut her teeth in the Eastern District, by far the most violent of the city's nine police precincts. Plus Holmes had been assigned to Eastern's highest-crime area: Post 323. Gang-related gunshots rang out so frequently, and Holmes encountered so many shooting victims, that at times she wondered if she'd secretly joined the Army Green Berets instead of the Baltimore City Police Department.

She had even been the recipient of several dreaded East Baltimore airmails—an innocent-sounding name for deadly chunks of concrete flung from the rooftops of low-income tenements onto police squad cars responding to calls. Holmes had been airmailed three different times, including an occasion when a roll of roofing tar shattered the windshield of her police vehicle, sending Holmes to the hospital to have glass slivers removed from her eyes and scalp.

Despite that, tenacious Thelma Holmes couldn't picture herself in any other line of work, regardless of protests from her parents and from boyfriends who begged her to quit police work, then faded into the distance when she wouldn't. Not to mention men too intimidated to make a pass once they found out how she put food on her table.

Within the police department, Holmes knew she was viewed as everything from an incompetent, quota-filling minority "two-for," to a ball-busting opportunist bitch, to the biggest slut to don the uniform of Baltimore's finest.

As long as she knew who she was and what she was about, and as long as her department heads knew, Holmes frankly couldn't give a rat's ass what anyone else thought.

Including Scott Donatelli, whose hostility and needling didn't surprise her. It was annoying as hell, but she could endure it. Like a thief in the night, she would steal knowledge and expertise Donatelli had taken years to accumulate, then wind up heading homicide before he realized what hit him.

I've got places to go, son. You ain't nothing more than a little goatee-wearing speed bump.

"Ever work an old homicide case before, Detective?" Donatelli asked out of the blue. They both knew the answer to that query, which was little more than another salvo in Donatelli's one-sided war.

"Nope. Been looking forward to getting one under my belt, though."

"We don't need the medical examiner to tell us somebody iced this lady," Donatelli said, gnawing at his trademark toothpick. "Two-to-one she was snuffed by someone she knew."

Holmes remained silent. Earlier in their relationship, she would have asked questions, stroked Donatelli's ego. But given the glacial chill that existed between them now, Holmes preferred to keep their exchanges to a minimum. He'd eventually divulge what she wanted to know anyway, without any apple-polishing on her part.

Donatelli was one prickly jerk, but Holmes had to admit that his street smarts were impeccable and he knew his way around a homicide investigation. The information and training she received from her partner were consistently first-rate—it was the stupid hazing Holmes could do without.

Confident of her ability to handle the Safe&Sound case with or without Donatelli, Holmes quietly broiled in the unforgiving sunshine, feeling greasy and sticky as beads of sweat crawled through her short, curly black hair.

Cutting his eyes, Donatelli quietly took in Holmes's unadorned beauty as they waited for the arrival of the "meat wagon," the van used by the medical examiner's office to transport corpses. If anything, Donatelli mused, Holmes's shiny, glistening skin made her appear even more exotic. And the ringlets of wet hair on the nape of her thick neck were sexy as hell.

Alarmed at the path his thoughts were taking, Donatelli chided himself for regarding a fellow detective in such unprofessional terms. All the more reason the two of them didn't need to be chasing bad guys together all over the city. The partner he really wanted to accompany him was Phil Gardner.

"Before we reenter Unit Twenty-five, dab at your head and neck," Donatelli barked. "Perspiration is the kiss of death at a crime scene."

Holmes turned abruptly, an incredulous look on her face. "Beg your pardon!" she snapped. "I really think you—"

The unexpected crack of a whip inches from her right ear startled Holmes, who spun around to see what was going on. Without warning, white-hot pain erupted from her right ear-lobe, as though she'd been attacked by a hornet.

"Oooooow!"

Pop-pop-pop-pop-pop-pop.

The shots rang out with impossible quickness, creating one long flatulent burst of sound instead of individual explo-sions of gunpowder.

Holmes instinctively dropped into a shooter's crouch, her back to Unit 25. The detective's Glock .40-caliber semiauto-matic service weapon had materialized in her right hand with-out her remembering having drawn it.

Pop-pop-pop.

Orange muzzle flashes near the top of the storage unit across the concrete alleyway from Unit 25 and two units down. Along with the barely visible head of someone lying prone, spraying shot after shot down on Holmes and Donatelli.

A primordial urge rose from her bowels that blotted out everything—thoughts, fear, even sound. It was a feeling—an emotion, really—of unalloyed power and one that was easily a hundred times stronger than any desire or craving she'd ever experienced: Thelma Holmes wanted to live.

She only had a fraction of a second to ensure that was the case and might never receive a second chance.

With practiced smoothness, Holmes raised her Glock pis-tol to eye level and drew a bead on her target. She coolly fired off three of her weapon's fifteen rounds, gently squeez-ing the gun's trigger, as she had practiced endless times at the shooting range.

The Glock's last two bullets zipped harmlessly through

the air, because Holmes's first shot bored into her assailant's cheek, just below his right eye. His head snapped over at an impossible angle and his shiny silver revolver leapt into the air liked a freshly hooked trout before clattering onto the concrete ten feet below.

Holmes took out the suspect just in time to save a tall, graying, black patrol officer who had been keeping civilians away from Unit 25 before the shooting started. Panic-stricken and standing bolt upright, he fired one wild round after another in the general direction of the shooter Holmes had already neutralized.

"Hold your fire, Patrolman!" she yelled, staying in her crouch and continuing to clutch her pistol. So much voltage was streaking through her body that her gun seemed to be weightless. Squatting, she swiveled 180 degrees, making sure no ambush awaited atop the blue storage units to her rear.

"I think he got me!" It was the eerily calm voice of Scott Donatelli. He lay with his back against the hot concrete, each leg jutting into the air and bent at the knee. A small hole on the left side of his tan cotton shirt indicated where the bullet had struck him.

Raising his head slightly, Donatelli dabbed his fingers at his side. He slowly brought his hand to his face, stared at it, then laid his head back on the concrete. "Shee-it!" he said quietly. "I don't fucking believe this! It hurts to breathe, Holmes."

Donatelli's right hand eased its death grip on his .40-caliber weapon, which he'd never fired.

"Stop talking, Scott. We'll have you out of here in a minute."

For some reason, Holmes recalled one of the hundreds of factoids she'd learned during police department first-aid training: *One-quarter of all chest injury victims die, often after reaching the hospital.* Quickly pushing that ugly thought out of her mind,

Holmes grabbed the handheld radio clipped to her thick leather belt. But she couldn't push the button to transmit a message: An embarrassing tremor had taken control of both of her hands.

Holmes turned toward the graying, uniformed patrol officer, who was still holding his pistol and standing zombielike in the alleyway, staring dumbly at Holmes.

"Whatcha waiting for?" she bellowed. "Key your mike and get an ambulance in here. Backup, too."

A few feet away lay the crumpled, convulsing body of Safe&Sound's manager, Joseph Dennis. A small sea of crimson surrounded his badly deformed head, which had been struck in the left temple by a copper-jacketed bullet.

Down the alleyway, Adele Jones had staggered about thirty feet from where Dennis was hit before collapsing against the metal door of Unit 16. A sloping line of smeared blood on the door bore mute testimony to the angle at which she had fallen.

She was still conscious, though extremely disoriented and becoming less lucid by the second. Her summery, nearly opaque blouse was soaked in blood and each time her chest rose, Holmes could hear air being pulled through a hole in Jones's chest wall. Holmes had learned about this in first-aid class, too—a sucking chest wound!

Finally rising from her crouch, Holmes sprinted toward the dazed-looking patrol officer, who had put out a call for help and was awaiting a response.

"Give me your shirt!" she barked at him.

"Huh?"

"Give me your shirt. Quickly!" Holmes waved her pistol for emphasis.

The veteran flatfoot, who was months from retirement and thought he had seen it all, numbly removed his sweaty dark blue uniform shirt. Under his shirt was a thick beige Kevlar flak jacket designed to protect against gunshot wounds.

Patrol officers wore them all the time, because of the volatile, unpredictable nature of beat work. But homicide detectives pretty much ignored them, figuring they had better odds of winning the lottery than of getting popped.

"Blood on your face," the old patrolman uttered in a robotic voice. "Your ear."

Holmes, who was already running to where Jones lay, didn't hear the comment. She wadded the cop's shirt into a tight ball as she ran and pressed it hard against Jones's chest, as she had seen numerous first-aid instructors do.

Her hands shook so badly that she had trouble maintaining pressure on Jones's chest. Tongues of fiery pain were starting to flicker through Holmes's earlobe and into her right cheek as she listened to the distant sound of approaching emergency sirens.

As she administered aid to Jones, Holmes began to pray with an intensity she'd never achieved in thirty-one years of living.

Among other things, she thanked God that the Baltimore City Police Department had stopped issuing 9mm handguns, opting instead for the more powerful .40-caliber piece that had just saved her life.

CHAPTER 6

W e had a little problem this morning . . ."
Feeling the air start to leak from his good mood, the man in the oak-paneled office removed the phone from his ear, dipped his head, and began massaging the bridge of his nose. He knew from Gregory's tone that a "little problem" was actually a full-blown fiasco. It had been a mistake to entrust this whole operation to Gregory, a horrible, horrible misjudgment.

"What kind of problem, Greg?" he murmured dejectedly, fully anticipating something horrific and unsettling. Something career-threatening.

"I took a shooter with me to Unit Twenty-five."

"Why on earth—why in God's name would you do that? What are you thinking about, man?"

"Because somebody found her and I needed to get rid of them."

It took a second to register that Gregory meant people had been shot. An already foul situation had escalated into shootings.

"Please don't tell me that anyone is dead or seriously injured. Please!"

"Four people." The tone, that of a contrite boy caught stealing cookies. "One is a cop. I know for a fact one is dead."

Great God almighty! Well, this had to be the end of the road. The acclaim and prestige had to end at some point—but like this?

"Who's dead, Greg? Who?"

"I think a homicide cop, two other people who found our secret, and my shooter."

For the first time since he'd been a snot-nosed youngster running the streets of Baltimore, the man in the oak-paneled, pastel-accented office felt totally helpless, vulnerable, and afraid. The media would be all over this thing, snapping up every shred of information to increase their ratings and sell newspapers.

They'll want answers and explanations for everything. They won't even care about Gregory, but they'll sure as hell want my scalp.

"Greg, why . . . how . . . At least tell me the cop isn't dead."

"I don't think he is. Could be, though."

With every answer the situation grew increasingly grim.

"Did anybody see you?"

"No. I don't think so."

If Gregory was subjected to a police interrogation, he'd last about half an hour before spilling everything. Not because he was a punk—the man had the heart of a lion. It's just that whenever Greg had to rely on wits instead of a gun or fists, he was akin to a man waging a sword fight with a butter knife.

"Greg, you have got to tell me exactly what happened. Or else I won't have any chance to get us out of this situation."

The man in the oak-paneled office listened in disbelief as Gregory recounted how his accomplice at Unit 25 had been shot in the head by a female cop, how Donatelli had been wounded in the side, how the side of Joseph Dennis's head had disappeared in an explosion of blood and bone, and how Adele Jones had staggered away while bleeding profusely from her chest.

A body count that started at one when the day dawned had now ballooned to five. What was there to say?

So the brothers remained silent for several seconds as Gregory listened to the slow, angry breathing on the other end of the line. He found that a hundred times worse than a tongue-lashing.

"Have you told me *everything*?"

"Yeah. You know what I know."

"Okay, listen to me carefully, Greg. Stay home—please don't leave the house. And don't call me from your cell phone again, okay?"

Without waiting for an answer, the man in the oak-paneled office hung up. He put his elbows on his desk and cradled his head in his hands. Although his office was dead quiet, he found it impossible to think.

Usually dependent on his secretary, Sheila, for making phone calls, this time he opened the bottom drawer of his massive desk and slowly pulled out the Yellow Pages. He flipped open to the "Funeral Homes" section and circled the phone number for Washington Funeral Home.

How did the saying go? A leader keeps his head when others are losing theirs?

The beauty of life was that no matter how bleak things appeared, there was at least one escape route.

The Washington Funeral Home was run by Hubert

Washington, a Harvard undergraduate classmate who'd opted to return to Baltimore and run his family's funeral home business. He and Hubert had been among the few specks of pepper in their 1970 Harvard graduating class and had remained reasonably close over the years. Even better, Hubert owed the man in the oak-paneled office a favor or two. Making him the best kind of friend to have—one who owed something.

The man in the oak-paneled office stood up and stretched, taking in the framed Harvard undergraduate and Yale law degrees adorning the walls. His career had been built on turning around bad situations, on making something out of nothing. That ability would let him neutralize the Unit 25 debacle before things got any further out of hand. It wouldn't be easy— in fact, it would be damned difficult. But it was doable.

The handsome, successful black man who took inordinate pride in the impressive plaques and certificates sprinkled throughout his office shuffled across the thick shag carpet and opened the door a crack. Seated at her desk just outside the door to his office, his middle-aged no-nonsense secretary, Sheila, was hard at work. She was busy preparing his schedule for the following week and didn't even notice him.

"Sheila, please hold my calls for the rest of the day. Cancel my appointments, too, for today and tomorrow. Thanks, dear heart."

The door was shut again; then a call was quietly placed to Washington Funeral Home. Even though black-on-black fratricide had the place running at full capacity and had inflated Hubert Washington's worth to seven figures, he'd likely be right there. Born dirt-poor, Hubert was one of those people who could never have too much money.

The phone only rang twice before, sure enough, Hubert answered. His pseudo-somber tone barely masked his eagerness to deal with another moneymaking passing. Or transition. Or whatever the latest euphemism for death was in the funeral business.

"Good afternoon, Washington Funeral Home. May I help you?"

"Hubert, what's shakin', baby?" the man in the oak-paneled office said with forced cheerfulness.

"Scooter," Washington replied, using a nickname that only old, dear friends knew, "that you, man? What's going on? Haven't heard from you much, lately. Too big to rub shoulders with us commoners these days?"

CHAPTER 7

Darryl Billups wasn't sure what jolted Yolanda most when he wandered back to their home at 10:00 A.M.—the odor of stale sinsemilla that trailed him or the fact that he'd stayed out all night.

Even so, Yolanda's behavior was strangely subdued. She calmly asked Darryl where he'd been and, seeing that he was in no mood to rationalize or otherwise explain his behavior, quickly dropped the subject.

With their communication breakdown now complete, the two of them moved warily throughout the house they shared, taking pains not to be in the same room at the same time. Little Jamal was still asleep, further accentuating the awkwardness Darryl and Yolanda felt around each other. In a world filled with so much unpleasantness, it didn't seem right that they had to feel ill at ease in their own home, each around the individual who was supposed to be his or her soul mate.

It wasn't that long ago that they couldn't wait to be in each other's presence. Now, they gathered themselves before entering the front door, wondering what negative maelstrom awaited. Cuddles, tickles, and playful giggles had given way to scowls and hurtful words. Even their sex life had an uninspired, by-the-numbers quality lately.

Darryl listened as Yolanda stomped around the kitchen, filling their house with the staccato rattle of plates and eating utensils being violently shoved into the sink. She wasn't washing dishes so much as wordlessly communicating her displeasure with Darryl. One of her classic passive/aggressive outbursts that he couldn't stand. And that she knew he couldn't stand.

Seated inside the guest room, which doubled as his office, Darryl made a silent vow to bring the tense, unhappy standoff to a close. Feeling an acute sense of dread, Darryl rose slowly and began to walk toward the kitchen when the soothing chimes of the kitchen telephone began to peal.

Before Darryl could return to the guest room, which had a desk phone in it, Yolanda had scampered from the sink to the kitchen wall phone. She mumbled something Darryl couldn't make out; then he heard the loud clatter of the telephone receiver banging against the wall as it bounced on its elastic cord like a bungee jumper.

"Phone!" she bellowed crossly.

Darryl stopped in his tracks, scarcely believing Yolanda's rude, belligerent behavior.

When he walked into the kitchen, the first thing that caught his eye was the phone receiver, still bouncing and alternately striking the floor and the wall. As Darryl stooped to pick it up, Yolanda never turned around from the sink. The floor near her slipper-clad feet glistened from splashes of erupting dishwater.

"Hello," Darryl said curtly.

"Hey, Darryl. Catch you at a bad time?" said kindly, even-tempered *Baltimore Herald* weekend metro editor Gary Birmingham. Gary had been the *Herald*'s religion reporter before segueing into management. Everyone had predicted he'd be too mild-mannered to ride herd over high-strung, egotistical reporters, but Gary was doing just fine.

"Naw, Gary. What's up?"

"We've got a breaking deal in Northwest Baltimore. Five people shot, including two city homicide cops." Even though Darryl was off on Saturdays, it was understood that he was expected to drop everything and cover major stories. The news business can be an all-consuming mistress.

"I'm on it, Gary. What's the address?"

"Thanks, Darryl," Birmingham said gratefully. "We've got a green reporter covering cops today and there's no way he can handle this. I've got him here working the phones, which he ain't too happy about."

Darryl gently replaced the phone in its wall-mounted cradle, tickled to have a legitimate excuse to get away from the house and Yolanda. He'd just as soon sprint through Hades wearing gasoline drawers than spend an additional second in his rapidly disintegrating relationship.

Yolanda must have sensed his relief, because she glared at him from the sink, slowly wiping her hands dry with a red-and-white checkered dishrag. "You always ready to run behind the white man to do his bidding. He say jump and you say, 'Hello! How high, Boss?' " she said, putting a mocking Step 'N' Fetchit tone in her voice.

Making a conscious effort not to respond, Darryl pulled off his soiled shirt. And steeled himself. He looked around at the kitchen, trying to memorize the little homey touches throughout, including the blue-and-white GOD BLESS THIS HOME plaque on the wall near the stove. The sweet, funny, considerate woman who'd placed that there had been run off by Sistah She-Devil.

"This isn't working, Yolanda," Darryl said in a monotone. "We need to split up and do our own thing." There! The topic they'd been tiptoeing around was finally out in the open. That's what all the drama was really all about, not Darryl's running behind the white man.

"I knew it!" Yolanda screeched. "You spend one night with some slut and you're ready to kick me and Jamal to the curb. I knew you was gonna do something fucked up like this. That's why me and Jamal movin' in with Boone. Jamal needs to be with his daddy—not some weak-ass punk."

A swift kick to the family jewels couldn't have been more hurtful. How long had she and Boone been talking!

After Yolanda dropped that H-bomb, there was really nothing more to say, so Darryl silently exited the kitchen. He walked into the bedroom hallway, made a left into the bathroom, and closed the door behind him.

How long had Yolanda and Boone been talking to each other—and where had they been talking? That question rattled around Darryl's brain the entire time he washed up in the sink, put on fresh clothes, and drove to the Safe&Sound on Reisterstown Road. "Yolanda, I am sorry I ever laid eyes on you—you witch!" he yelled as he drove, keeping his eyes on traffic. A motorist in a nearby car stared at Darryl oddly, averting her eyes to avoid eye contact with the unhinged black man ten feet away.

Darryl was still about half a mile away from the Safe&Sound when he spotted a sea of flashing blue police beacons flanking the storage facility. Half the city's police force seemed to be milling about, looking tense and officious. Cops tend to be edgy as hell when one of their own takes a bullet. Darryl knew that from experience. Emotions would be running high and the natural tendency cops have to be clannish and suspicious would be more pronounced than usual.

Before reaching the commotion surrounding the Safe&Sound, Darryl turned right onto a side street and parked. Unlike what he was experiencing at home, the madness at the Safe&Sound would unfold predictably. He would interview people, take notes, drive to the *Baltimore Herald*, and write a story. For the next few hours at least, his brain wouldn't be weighed down with thoughts of Yolanda or Jamal. Or Boone. Or the Winslows. Or Camille.

Yellow police tape fluttered from a blue chain-link fence, circling the Safe&Sound complex. Standing behind the tape, which spanned a front gate large enough to accommodate trucks and rental vans, were two uniformed cops who seemed thrilled to be sunbathing in their dark uniforms on an August morning.

Knowing he probably wouldn't get far, Darryl walked toward them, hoping to flash his laminated press pass and schmooze his way into the Safe&Sound compound. He was still thirty feet away when one cop nudged the other. Both nodded at Darryl, which was an encouraging sign.

He was something of a minor celebrity within the Baltimore City Police Department, thanks to having helped close two major homicide cases. The first involved a plot to bomb the NAACP's national headquarters, which had led to three deaths. In the second highly publicized case, Darryl helped nail a deranged woman who was killing middle-class black victims in Baltimore and Atlanta.

Because he'd worked closely with the cops on both occasions, some police officers mistakenly viewed Darryl as a police cheerleader. Actually, he wasn't friend or foe, just an aggressive reporter ever on the prowl for a juicy story. But if the perception that Darryl was a "good guy" helped him gain access, that was okay with him.

"What's shakin', fellas?" Darryl said easily. Just another rank-and-file guy shooting the breeze with the troops.

"Aft'noon, Mr. Billups," replied one of the cops, the short, muscular white one who'd alerted his buddy to Darryl's approach.

Darryl made a show of slowly easing his wallet from his back pocket and flipping out his press pass. Then he cracked the wallet open a sliver, enough for the two cops to glimpse the wad of five- and one-dollar bills within.

"So what's the price of admission?" Darryl said, grinning and drawing an appreciative chuckle from his uniformed audience.

"Hold on a second," the white cop said, taking off his hat and wiping his glistening face with a hairy forearm. "I'll get the detective in charge."

He returned with the second ranking officer of Baltimore's homicide unit, Lt. Tuck Anders. His prematurely gray crew cut made Anders appear sixty-five instead of fifty. As he was not a particularly accomplished detective or a skillful backroom operator, Anders's rise within the homicide department had surprised Darryl.

Anders had a queer habit of not making eye contact or responding immediately when spoken to. At first, Darryl wondered if Anders's behavior was a personal slight, but he soon noticed that everyone got the same queer response.

"Must be a real shit storm for you to be here, Lieutenant," Darryl said amiably. Anders's gaze remained fixed on something over Darryl's shoulder. "What went down here this afternoon?"

Still no response. Anders made a fist and rubbed a knuckle against his right temple, sending an avalanche of dandruff fluttering onto the dark collar of his long-sleeve dress shirt.

"Can I come inside for a quick look, Lieutenant?"

Anders looked at Darryl as if seeing him for the first time. "Darryl, we've got about ten police technicians tearing this place apart, looking for evidence," he said sternly. "Got a stiff in one of the units that somebody felt real protective of."

"Male, female? And what happened to the people who got shot, including your guys?"

"Got three capped civilians, including a perp, with two deceased," Anders said brusquely. "The wounded detectives are Scott Donatelli and Thelma Holmes. We should have a statement in an hour," Anders added, turning to walk back inside.

Darryl shuddered because he and Donatelli had worked closely on the Baltimore/Atlanta serial killing case and had grudgingly earned each other's grudging respect in the process.

"Scott okay?" Darryl blurted.

Anders shrugged and continued toward the crimson-splattered concrete surrounding Unit 25. The detective was back inside the Safe&Sound complex and out of sight when Darryl remembered he hadn't confirmed the gender of the body that apparently had triggered all the mayhem. "Dammit!"

Tucking his slim reporter's notebook in his back pocket, Darryl walked briskly away from the front gate. Weekly workouts at the athletic club had put 175 well-proportioned pounds on his five-foot-ten frame. As he walked, Darryl examined the blue chain-link fence around the Safe&Sound with ease, calculating how difficult it would be to scale.

After walking about fifty yards, Darryl turned left and continued to walk, still closely examining the chain-link fence. It was roughly seven feet high and probably extended 200 yards into the distance from the point where Darryl had turned the corner.

Do I really want to do this?

Before he knew it, Darryl's comfortable black work shoes were digging into the fence; then he was dropping toward the concrete on the other side. A jolt of pain ran through Darryl's right ankle as soon as he made contact with the ground, a not so gentle reminder that he was thirty-four, not fourteen.

"Ow!"

Crouching, Darryl moved quickly toward a row of storage units. Feeling strangely exhilarated, he squatted and pushed his back up against the doors of one of the storage units.

He looked left and right and was stunned to find himself alone on that particular side of the Safe&Sound complex. Darryl immediately stood up and began strutting in the general direction of Unit 25 as if he owned the place.

As soon as Darryl rounded a corner, the next row of self-storage units was swarming with uniformed and plainclothes cops. The first one he happened upon was Tuck Anders, who had his back to Darryl and was casually talking to a couple of colleagues.

Trying to walk neither too fast nor too slow, Darryl went by Anders, who never turned as Darryl went by. Everyone except him had police badges pinned to their uniform shirts or clipped to their belts, yet no one stopped him as he marched toward Unit 25 and strode inside.

The unreality of the situation made Darryl feel like laughing his ass off, but he maintained a poker face, even nodding at a police technician busily taking photographs of what appeared to be black roofing plastic with a 35mm camera.

The first thing Darryl immediately noticed about the interior of Unit 25 was the time-capsule quality of everything inside it. All the appliances, clothing, and furniture seemed out-of-date—it looked to be stuff that was bought during the 1970s or 1980s.

A big wood cabinet television set that looked to be on loan from the Smithsonian sat off to one side. Darryl also noticed an eight-track stereo system—when was the last time anyone had played an eight-track?

Peering at a stack of *Ebony* magazines near his feet, Darryl noticed the date of the top issue: April 1984. He wanted to move the stack to see what dates were on the other magazines.

Several other police employees were also standing in the general vicinity, so Darryl gravitated toward where the action appeared to be. As he got closer, he could see that the plastic was peeled back to reveal the remains of a female human body.

The roofing plastic had acted as a barrier against beetles, maggots, and rodents, leaving the shrunken corpse surprisingly well-preserved. It was surrounded by a quarter inch of white powder, which had been sprinkled liberally inside the roofing plastic and on the victim's body. It was lime that had been placed on the body to quiet the riotous odors that emanate from a rotting body. Unbeknownst to the killer, calcium oxide not only combats the smell of putrefaction but also, in many instances, retards the process of decomposition.

The corpse of Unit 25 mirrored that of famed Irish author Oscar Wilde, who was buried in quicklime in 1900. When his remains were unearthed nine years later, not only was Wilde's corpse in excellent shape, but he had actually grown hair.

Likewise, the poor soul in Unit 25 had noteworthy hair follicles, flowing, medium-length brown tresses that appeared to have been combed minutes earlier. Despite being clad in only a white blood-stained bra and white panties, the lonely occupant of Unit 25 emanated a quiet dignity that transcended death.

Still, Darryl felt pity for the unnamed victim. He couldn't help but feel sorry for some soul who'd been stashed away in a self-storage unit like an outmoded piece of furniture. Regardless of who this woman was and what she had done, she deserved better than that, Darryl thought, writing furiously the entire time.

A spectacular bracelet with an eighteen-karat white gold mounting and fifty-six princess-cut diamonds adorned the deceased's right wrist, while a two-karat gold, platinum, and diamond engagement ring was perched on the poor soul's left hand.

Darryl scribbled all this down in his narrow spiral-back reporter's notebook, not daring to make eye contact with anyone else. Feeling that he had pushed his luck to ridiculous limits, the bold *Baltimore Herald* reporter slowly closed his notebook, stuck it in his back pocket, and sauntered out of Unit 25.

Darryl left in the opposite direction from the one he'd entered, not wanting to chance an encounter with Tuck Anders. Still carrying himself as if he were the lord of all he surveyed, Darryl fought an overwhelming urge to run and casually walked between a row of blue storage unit doors that seemed as though it would go on forever.

When he reached the end, Darryl turned right and walked about forty feet to the blue fence. As had been the case before, not a single cop was in sight. Frantically clambering up the fence now, Darryl jumped to the other side and landed on a stretch of grass abutting the sidewalk, hurting his ankle anew.

Darryl half limped the half block to where his car was parked, praying not to hear a cop bellow, "Halt!" before he got there. But no one yelled out or even looked at him before.

Withdrawing the ignition key from his pocket, Darryl slid it into the car door, and his shoulders slumped with relief.

CHAPTER 8

Detective Thelma Holmes grunted as the business end of a syringe full of Lidocaine met the exposed nerve endings of her torn right earlobe. The emergency room physician working on Holmes had warned her she'd feel a "pinch" as the needle numbed her damaged flesh. Instead, Holmes felt as though someone had hooked a 10,000-volt electric line to her ear. She dug her fingernails into the palms of her hands until the fire mercifully faded, replaced by nothingness.

She glared at the doctor working on her, an East Indian native with an unpronounceable name, who appeared to be in his late twenties.

"I'll give that five minutes to take full effect; then I'll put in a few stitches," he said in a singsong voice.

Thelma nodded and shifted her gaze to the blood pressure cuff on her right arm. The tough detective had despised needles since she was one year old. The twenty-first century had dawned, so why was Western medicine still using primitive metal tubes to puncture people's skin?

Holmes's thoughts abruptly flashed to her partner, Scott Donatelli, who might be dying or dead while she was being treated for a minor flesh wound. A mental image of the woman who had been shot at the Safe&Sound came next, followed by the poor man whose head had erupted into a geyser of red mist a millisecond before he tumbled to the ground. Then Holmes frowned as she remembered the dirtbag she'd nailed on the roof at the Safe&Sound.

She had worked for years on the rough-and-tumble streets of East Baltimore without having to fire her side arm but had shot and killed a man within months of becoming a homicide detective! It was a running joke among street patrolmen that homicide detectives probably couldn't even find their weapons in an emergency, much less fire them properly.

Even though she had hoped to never discover for herself, Thelma Holmes had always wondered what it would be like to send a high-velocity projectile crashing into another person's body, causing so much damage that life ended.

She'd just had that experience an hour earlier and was surprised to be feeling vaguely elated.

Not over the death of her assailant—Holmes was simply happy to be alive! She'd gone *mano a mano* with a madman and had prevailed. She really didn't give a damn whether her attacker had died quickly or writhed in agony, ascended into heaven or nose-dived straight to hell.

Bottom line, she was going to see her parents tonight and still had a chance—although it was getting admittedly slimmer with each passing day—to eventually have a husband and snot-nosed kids.

Any sympathy she could have felt for her assailant was snuffed out when he creased her ear with a bullet moving at supersonic speed.

Holmes's reverie was interrupted by a blond nurse who popped her head through the green hospital curtain surrounding Holmes's emergency room enclosure. "Got a visitor—you decent?"

"I'm fine," Holmes replied, curious who her mystery guest might be. "Come in."

The curtain parted and homicide lieutenant Tuck Anders strode into the enclosure, actually making eye contact for a change. Holmes regarded him coolly, on guard in the presence of a police department higher-up.

"They say you probably saved the lives of two officers at the storage depot in West Baltimore," Anders said, briskly shaking Holmes's hand. "Damn nice work, Detective! I'm going to put you in for a commendation."

Who cares about commendations right now? If you want to show me some love, put it in my paycheck!

Holmes shook Anders's hand primly, suddenly resenting his intrusion. What did Anders want? She had already given two statements about what had happened at the Safe&Sound and preferred not to go through that ordeal again.

"Of course you'll be on administrative leave when you come back," Anders said. "That's standard procedure in fatal-force investigations." He remained in front of Holmes, giving her a "thumbs-up" sign and grinning like an idiot. Holmes decided at that instant that she liked the aloof Anders a helluva lot better.

With perfect timing, a youngish-looking male physician's assistant breezed through the green curtain carrying a small chrome tray filled with medical equipment—a curved Kelly clamp, straight surgical scissors, curved iris scissors, smooth forceps, four types of surgical sutures, aloe vera gel, bandages, gauze, and a No. 11 scalpel alongside a No. 15.

Holmes frowned—didn't she merit a full-fledged doctor?

"Whoa—I'm outta here," Anders said, to Holmes's relief. Like practically everyone else in homicide, she didn't hold Anders in particularly high esteem.

Ignoring Anders's departure, the physician's assistant was preoccupied with his suture kit as he selected the best tools for sewing Holmes's ear back together.

"How does my ear look?" Holmes asked, reaching up to touch it before realizing what she was doing. Lidocaine was worth its weight in gold.

"Actually, it doesn't look that bad," answered the physician's assistant, who had N. MYERS on his nameplate. "You won't be wearing an earring in that lobe for a while, but it's not too bad."

Opting for 3-0 Chromic gut sutures, the PA went to work stitching Holmes's right ear.

She initially watched him closely, to see if he went about his work confidently, with sure, steady hands. Seeing that was the case, Holmes allowed her mind to wander.

You almost bought it today, girl! You nearly got killed.

If her assailant had aimed another two or three inches to the right, the bullet would have gone into Holmes's eye. Then a body bag would have been required, not a suture kit.

Myers abruptly stopped sewing Holmes's ear back together and looked at her quizzically. "You okay, Detective?" he asked, glancing at her shaking hands. Holmes quickly locked her fingers together, embarrassed that her mind could handle a brush with death, but her body apparently couldn't.

"I'm fine," she replied. Which was a lie, because with her

body finally starting to slow its adrenaline output, Thelma Holmes was starting to feel profoundly fatigued. "Are we almost finished?"

"We're not finished, but we almost were!" a joyous male voice boomed from behind the green hospital curtain and a bare-chested Scott Donatelli burst through, smiling. For an instant, Holmes wondered if she was dreaming.

Donatelli's sport jacket and his shirt hung loosely off his shoulders, and an angry-looking black-and-purple bruise, roughly the size of a cantaloupe, was on the left side of his chest, midway between his belly button and breastbone.

"Scott!"

Walking gingerly, he approached Holmes, grabbed her cheeks, and placed a big kiss on her oily forehead. "Thanks, Holmes," he said gratefully.

"I thought you'd be in an operating room!" Holmes said, keeping her head still as the PA finished up his work.

"You know how Anders always nags us about slapping on a lightweight bullet-proof vest?" Donatelli said in a quiet voice. "Well, I started wearing one about two weeks ago . . . " Donatelli's voice trailed off.

"He was only firing a .22-caliber," Donatelli continued, sounding awestruck. "The perp you took out was only sixteen, Holmes."

She raised her hand, a signal for Donatelli and the physician's assistant to stop. "Run that by me again—he was sixteen?"

Donatelli nodded.

"And he's dead?"

Another nod.

She had shot a baby! What in God's name was a sixteen-year-old doing firing on police officers investigating an old homicide case? And what about that poor man who had half of his head blown off? He sure wasn't hit by some popgun .22-caliber.

Despite learning her assailant's age, Holmes remained unmoved. *If you're eight to eighty, blind, crippled, or crazy, and you come at me with a gun I'm gonna take you out.*

PART

DANCING WITH SHADOWS

I don't like short-term solutions; they can come back and bite you in the behind later.

—CAROLINE R. WHITE

CHAPTER 9

Baltimore police homicide detectives and crime lab techni-cians took their time removing the contents of Safe&Sound Unit 25, dusting for fingerprints, and spraying luminol, a chemi-cal that shows where blood has been spilled by glowing when put under an ultraviolet light.

It was a little after 9:00 P.M. by the time they'd finished re-moving household items and got around to examining the body of the unidentified black female who'd been entombed there.

The Safe&Sound office at Reisterstown Road was turned upside down in an effort to find out who'd rented Unit 25 and when. But four police investigators only managed to frustrate themselves after a futile eight-hour search of business records that had them cussing and muttering to themselves.

They all agreed, however, to return early the next day

and comb through the office three more times, if necessary. Two of their own had been shot, so they were ready to move heaven and earth if it would help collar the scumbag responsible for the shootings.

From police headquarters in downtown Baltimore, a call was placed to Safe&Sound's home office in Waukeegan, Illinois, so that the company's computerized files could be searched. But the police were stymied once again, because Safe&Sound had only started computerizing customer data in 1994. By all appearances, the homicide victim at the Baltimore Safe&Sound had been there at least since the 1980s.

So the cops found themselves back at square one. The tarpaulin surrounding the dead woman at the Safe&Sound was carefully checked for trace evidence, then fully removed to reveal "Lady S&S," as detectives had already dubbed her.

Although no one said a word, the same thought was on everyone's mind: What secret did this black woman hold that had brought about the shootings of five people?

More than 100 photographs were taken of Lady S&S from every conceivable angle, to the point that it looked as though someone were setting off disco strobe lights inside Unit 25.

When her first and only photo shoot was over, a pair of latex-encased hands carefully removed Lady S&S's bra and panties. Scrapings were taken from beneath her fingernails and two were even clipped off and placed in a plastic evidence bag, in case hair or skin from her assailant was lodged beneath them.

Then two workers from the Maryland Medical Examiner's Office hoisted Lady S&S from her resting place and slipped her into a white plastic body bag. She was so light, they didn't bother to fetch the collapsible gurney inside their state van. Instead, they walked about twenty feet to where the death wagon awaited and unceremoniously shoved Lady S&S inside for a fifteen-minute trip to 111 Penn Street, an unremarkable three-story brick-and-granite structure just off Pratt Street and a long fly ball from Orioles Park at Camden Yards.

On a brick outer wall of 111 Penn Street, highlighted by two floodlights, were black block letters: FORENSIC MEDICAL CENTER, STATE OF MARYLAND. The van carrying Lady S&S turned into the parking lot and onto a sloping concrete ramp that led to the building's basement level. At the bottom of the ramp was a closed metal door monitored by a remote-controlled television camera.

To the left of the door were a wall-mounted intercom speaker and a doorbell with a small black-and-white sign beneath: PUSH BUTTON TO CALL INVESTIGATOR. The driver of Lady S&S's van ignored the sign. Instead, he removed a passkey from his pants pocket and pushed the key into a slot near the corrugated metal door. It immediately lurched skyward and the van inched into the maw of 111 Penn Street, propelled along by the muffled cheers of Camden Yards faithful.

" 'Yea, though I walk through the valley of the shadow of death . . .' " the driver droned solemnly, trying to get a reaction out of his partner, who merely yawned and peeked at his watch.

The two chauffeurs for the Dearly Departed stopped inside a chilly underground garage/loading dock area wide enough to accommodate six medical examiner vans, or hearses, sitting abreast. The men were nearing the end of a "Fat Tuesday" workday when they'd lifted a succession of obese corpses weighing 200 pounds or more. So they were relieved to encounter Lady S&S, who couldn't have weighed more than fifty pounds thanks to the lack of fluid in her body.

Using one hand apiece, they snatched up Lady S&S's body bag as though it were a mail sack and slung it onto a slab-sided metal gurney.

"Careful, gentlemen, careful," droned a balding black autopsy assistant who had been standing nearby in his dark blue surgical scrubs as he monitored the drivers. He pushed a wall-mounted button and a pair of double doors leading to the medical examiner's autopsy suites slowly swung open like a giant mechanical clamshell.

"They've been waiting for her," the autopsy assistant said to no one in particular. "She went to the head of the autopsy line because of those shootings. They plan to cut her open tonight and do some preliminary stuff; then the old man is going to do a thorough slice job tomorrow morning."

Around the Maryland Medical Examiner's Office, "old man" was a reference to Chief Medical Examiner Harold Roth, who was actually only in his forties.

"I better get back to work," the autopsy assistant said. "See you guys later." Limping slightly, he pushed the gurney holding Lady S&S out of the garage area and in the direction of the building's two basement-level "chop shops."

One suite was for dead people whose bodies carried contagious diseases or had undergone decomposition. Their suite had a separate ventilation system that made sure unpleasant odors and diseases didn't spread through the rest of the building.

Everything else was handled in an adjoining suite, which had glass windows and didn't look much different from a hospital operating room.

Lady S&S was rolled past both suites into a room containing a large, floor-mounted stainless-steel scale. She was slipped out of her body bag and placed back on the surgical gurney, which was then rolled onto the scale. The weight of the twenty-five-pound gurney was subtracted from a weight of seventy-eight pounds.

Then Lady S&S was rolled into a cavernous intake refrigerator where she would lie in repose for about half an hour, until an assistant medical examiner wheeled her into a chop shop to collect some tissues for toxicology. Then Lady S&S would be trundled back into the intake refrigerator, to await the arrival of Dr. Roth in the morning.

NOTHING FOCUSES THE MIND like writing a story a few hundred thousand people will eagerly begin to devour the minute they pick up the morning paper. Especially when that bad boy has to be written in a couple of hours while an anxious editor hovers nearby, silently exhorting you to work even faster.

That's the position Darryl Billups found himself in on the *Baltimore Herald*'s fifth-floor newsroom. A sculptor putting the finishing touches on a masterpiece, Darryl chipped away at the *Herald*'s lead story, knocking off a cliché here, smoothing out a transition there.

Whatever he added or took away, the nagging perfectionist was never satisfied. One thing was certain—he would never be totally comfortable with whatever he wrote regardless of how long he had to write it.

He worked with the realization that the entire paper was depending on him to do his job with blazing speed and with accuracy and flair, too! The adrenaline rush that came from trying to juggle those demands was what daily journalism was all about.

Darryl smiled as he massaged his story, thinking about his little secret. Namely, that working as a reporter was so gratifying, he'd practically do it for free. That was the main reason he'd quit his editorial position six months ago, confounding the paper's other black journalists. Darryl understood their concern over one of the paper's few black editors voluntarily stepping down. But he simply wasn't cut out to sit behind a desk every day, wearing a stupid suit, while reporters went out and ran down stories. Like them, Darryl was a hunter-gatherer, not someone who was content to clean and cook the prey after it was dragged back to the *Herald*. He was happiest chasing fire trucks, poring over homicide cases, and trying to root out police corruption.

Darryl stopped typing and began to reread his story. Without thinking about it, he tugged at a corner of his mustache, a habit when the deadline dragon needed to be slain. "You about finished?" weekend metro editor Gary Birmingham asked, sounding anxious.

"Yeah, give me five, okay?"

"No problem, Darryl," Birmingham said, staring at his watch.

Darryl didn't even notice. Slouching behind the walls of his gray cubicle, he tugged contentedly at his mustache. The Safe&Sound deal was fascinating, but it was also frustrating.

Who was this woman found inside Unit 25? The cops said she appeared to be a black woman in her thirties, something Darryl had already surmised from the victim's hair. And why was a sixteen-year-old shooting at police officers?

The cop had IDed the kid as Alonzo Ellis. He had a fairly extensive criminal record—mainly shoplifting, car theft, and the like, nothing hinting that homicide was just over the horizon.

"Is it soup yet, Darryl?" Gary Birmingham again, who was starting to pluck Darryl's nerves. No way five minutes had passed! A check of the newsroom clock showed that it was actually fifteen minutes. Time seemed to elapse much faster than normal when a deadline had to be met.

"Sending it your way now," Darryl said, pushing a button that transferred his Safe&Sound story to Birmingham's computer. Not only was it a juicy front-page read for the *Herald*'s Sunday readers, but it had also allowed Darryl to totally immerse himself and not think once about Yolanda.

Darryl's cubicle was overrun with documents and books,

like every other messy, chaotic cubicle in the newsroom. But tonight, because he was in no rush to return home, the disarray was intolerable. So he systematically went through every stack of paper and shelved every book, meticulously sorting and throwing out half the stuff he'd accumulated. It was midnight when Darryl finished.

Sighing, he picked up his tape recorder and notebook and began to trudge toward the fifth-floor elevator. After the doors closed, he simply stood inside without pushing any buttons, breathing in the lubricating oil odor that always seemed to be inside the elevator.

Placing his hands on his hips, Darryl arched his back and could feel little tugs and pulls where his muscles had knotted up from being pressed against his uncomfortable office chair. Then the sound of miniature firecrackers rang out inside the elevator as Darryl methodically cracked each of his knuckles, a giveaway to his underlying nervousness.

Only then did Darryl get around to pushing the elevator button for the first floor, followed by the buttons for the second, third, and fourth floors—Darryl was taking the scenic route tonight. His actions over the last two hours had been the personification of procrastination, but Darryl was simply in no mood for a confrontation of any kind.

The elevator obediently stopped at each floor, revealing an empty, darkened hallway the first three times its doors eased open.

Even with those little detours, the first floor still arrived too quickly. Strolling into the lobby, Darryl chatted up a bored-looking night watchman and began shooting the breeze about typical male stuff—the Baltimore Ravens and Toni Braxton.

Darryl was badly tempted to start talking about his situation with Yolanda. But his intensely private nature overwhelmed his desire to get some badly needed feedback about his relationship.

So instead, he engaged in a brief superficial conversation, then headed toward the *Herald*'s parking lot, where his black coupe awaited.

Okay, let's get this deal over with.

In ten minutes Darryl was standing on his porch, sliding a door key into the front lock. A light from the kitchen shone through the living room window. Bracing himself, Darryl turned his key and pushed open the front door.

But the only thing he heard was the steady drip-drip of the leaky faucet in the kitchen that he'd been meaning to fix. As he pivoted toward the living room, Darryl immediately noticed that the landscape had been dramatically altered.

"Hey!"

The modern green leather sofa he and Yolanda had purchased together was missing, as was the big-screen television they made alternating payments on.

"Yolanda!"

Walking toward the hallway leading to his and Yolanda's bedroom, Darryl was surprised to find the bedroom door closed. But when he gave the cold brass doorknob a clockwise twist, the door wouldn't budge—it was locked!

Darryl raced toward the kitchen, where he and Yolanda hid bedroom keys from the prying eyes and hands of Jamal, her young son. Darryl fished one of the gold-colored keys from its hiding place in the silverware drawer and sprinted back to his bedroom.

No light came from beneath the bedroom door, so Darryl opened it slowly before snapping on the light. All of Yolanda's clothes were gone from her side of the closet and the army of toiletry items she kept on the dresser also was missing.

Darryl walked briskly into Jamal's bedroom. All of his little buddy's clothes were absent, as were his toys. Yolanda and Jamal had hightailed it—probably to Boon's—while Darryl had been at work.

Stunned, Darryl walked through the house, cataloging things that disappeared in the wake of Yolanda's departure. Most of the items in their house belonged to him, so he took his time moving from room to room, hoping that Yolanda hadn't done him in. To her credit, she had taken only things she could honestly lay claim to, with the exception of a toaster oven she knew damn well was his.

In the middle of inventorying the kitchen, Darryl spied a sheet of lined paper on the kitchen table. His heart stopped when he saw something glistening on top of the note.

Sitting under the engagement ring he'd given Yolanda was a note in her handwriting. Darryl forced himself to pick up the letter and read it. The scent of Yolanda's perfume wafted from the paper, making Darryl feel inexplicably heartsick.

DARRYL

I just couldn't take it anymore. We both tried but were diferent people. There was too much pain here and only a little bit of fun and laughing. And loving.

Me and Jamal are at my sister LaToya's house. Please do not try to contact us because you know Jamal loves you. It would not be good for his head and would only hurt him more.

It didn't end too good between us, but I will always feel something for you.

YOLANDA

Darryl eased his five-foot-ten frame into one of the oak chairs at the kitchen table and continued to hold Yolanda's letter. After a month of mutual torture, it should have been the answer to his prayers.

So how come his chest felt so heavy that Darryl could barely rise to his feet?

DEAD PEOPLE don't make noises, so what was all that tapping about near the intake refrigerator in the basement of the Maryland Medical Examiner's Office? The autopsy assistant scheduled to work the midnight shift had called in sick, so no one else should be on the basement floor at three-thirty in the morning.

Assistant Medical Examiner Dr. Jesus Estrada smiled as he went to investigate. The plumbing in the intake refrigerator had a mind of its own at times, happily gurgling Freon and emitting pops and hisses as though possessed. The unit kept its inhabitants cold, though, which was all that really mattered.

When Estrada had gotten to a point about ten feet from the refrigerator's huge, brushed-aluminum door, the tapping mysteriously stopped. "Stop the racket, amigos!" Dr. Estrada yelled out, laughing.

He turned on his heel and immediately collided with a hulking spectral figure dressed in black from head to toe. Yelping, Dr. Estrada instinctively threw up both hands and backpedaled like mad, crashing into the side of the massive refrigeration unit.

Dr. Estrada was so rattled, it took him a couple of seconds to realize he'd encountered a huge black man wearing a black leather trench coat—on a warm August night. The man also had panty hose over his face. Dr. Estrada forced himself to remain calm in order to remember as many details as possible.

"How did you get in here?" Dr. Estrada snapped, looking past the intruder to a nearby doorway leading to a stairwell and calculating whether or not he could make it without being intercepted. Sensing this, the figure in black took two quick feline steps to his left, blocking the potential escape route.

"I got friends in high places," the man replied in a deep, growling voice. "What time the next shift get in?"

"They'll be here any second," Dr. Estrada bluffed, thinking how ironic it would be if he perished in the basement of the Maryland Medical Examiner's Office.

"Don't play games with me," the intruder said darkly as he reached into his coat and calmly withdrew the biggest, blackest handgun Dr. Estrada had ever seen. "Anything down here worth dying for, Doc?"

"Uh, no," Dr. Estrada gasped in a small voice.

"Like I said—what time does the next shift get in?"

Now the gun was pointed directly at Dr. Estrada's head. He barely breathed, fearing the sudden appearance of an orange flash that would be the last thing he would ever see.

"They get in at eight."

The big fellow in the black trench coat thrust out an arm, his gaudy silver wristwatch to flashing into view. "Five hours from now," he said mysteriously. A horrible thought crossed Dr. Estrada's mind—perhaps this monster had sodomy *and* death on his agenda. If that was the case, Dr. Estrada preferred immediate death, *gracias*.

"Just go ahead and shoot me," he blurted, to the wonderment of his assailant.

"What you talkin' 'bout?" he boomed. "Stop trippin' and help me find the Safe&Sound woman."

Dr. Estrada sighed loudly. He'd gladly ID every stiff in the joint—and tell their life stories, too—if that's what it took to remain alive.

"She's in here," he said, reaching for the sturdy handle on the intake refrigerator's mammoth door. It felt massive and cool to his touch and Dr. Estrada pulled the door open with exaggerated slowness, lest a sudden move result in a bullet in his spine.

The corpse from Unit 25 lay just inside the doorway. A light blue sheet covered the dead woman's body, except for the big toe on her left foot, which had a toe tag looped around it.

"Right here," Dr. Estrada said, pointing toward the gurney holding Lady S&S. "Let me go, please. I can't ID you—I haven't seen your face."

"Shaddup and pull the sheet back!"

A string of ridiculously cheerful musical notes suddenly split the frigid air inside the intake refrigerator. The gunman reached into his pocket and pulled out a dainty-looking yellow cellular phone.

"Yeah?" he growled. The man in the oak-paneled office was on the other end, micromanaging things from afar. As usual. "Uh-huh, uh-huh. Look, I'm gettin' the body now. Let me handle my business—you handle *yours*." That last directive was spoken with such vehemence that Dr. Estrada flinched.

The dainty phone was snapped back in half like a clamshell and returned to its resting place.

In the short time it took to complete that conversation, Dr. Estrada had pulled back the sheet covering Lady S&S, who stared up at the gunman with sightless, accusatory eyes. Seemingly transfixed, he totally ignored Dr. Estrada and carelessly lowered his handgun to his side.

He walked up to the metal gurney holding Lady S&S and gently touched her remains, like a lover caressing his soul mate's face. The interior of the refrigerator went blurry and began to dance.

Despite the passage of nearly two decades, despite the fact that Lady S&S was mutilated and lifeless, he seemed to feel something for her. A single tear flowed from the gunman's right eye and coursed through the stocking covering his head.

Dr. Estrada watched dumbfounded, not daring to utter a word.

"Find a body bag and put her in it," the gunman commanded with a sniffle, roughly wiping his stocking-covered face with the back of a leather-gloved hand. Dr. Estrada quickly complied, then stood to one side of the gurney holding Lady S&S.

"Take off your belt, Doc."

"Huh?"

"What part of that don't you understand? Take off your goddamned belt."

Sure that death was mere seconds away and resigned to meeting his Maker, Dr. Estrada did as he was told and gently laid his belt in his assailant's huge outstretched hand. Then came an odd thought—which of his colleagues would perform his autopsy?

"Now turn around and put your hands behind your back."

Dr. Estrada meekly complied, silently praying that when the end came, it would be fast and without discomfort. That hope evaporated when his captor bound his wrists tightly enough to restrain King Kong.

"Stay inside the refrigerator and *be quiet*. Holler and you're dead."

The gunman closed the wide-eyed assistant medical examiner inside the cavernous intake refrigerator and shut the door. "Stay cool, Doc."

The gunman eased the big black handgun back into his waistband. He paused momentarily beside the gurney and the white body bag sitting atop it. It pained him to be reunited with her in such a heartbreaking manner.

"You ain't deserve this, baby. You ain't deserve this," he droned over and over. Her death had been so undignified, so frenzied. A queen didn't deserve to be butchered like some slaughterhouse hog. A simple truth forever lost on his brother, the asshole micromanager.

Her gurney was solemnly wheeled past the twin autopsy suites and out the double doors opening onto the garage.

A gleaming, cream-colored Cadillac hearse with gold Old English letters on either side—𝔚𝔞𝔰𝔥𝔦𝔫𝔤𝔱𝔬𝔫 𝔉𝔲𝔫𝔢𝔯𝔞𝔩 𝔥𝔬𝔪𝔢— awaited, its rear cargo area open for the passenger to come. The white plastic body bag bearing Lady S&S was lovingly placed in the back of the hearse; then the rear door was eased shut.

The gurney was pushed off to the side and it rolled away slowly in motion, stopping when it hit a far wall. Then Lady S&S's chauffeur walked toward the corrugated metal gate hiding the ramp leading to Pratt Street. He jabbed a red wall button near the gate which slowly eased skyward, creaking mournfully the entire time.

"Let's get out of here, baby. Time to go home."

The hearse was shifted into gear and driven slowly out of the basement of the Maryland Medical Examiner's Office, as though part of a funeral procession. The hearse made an immediate left turn onto Pratt Street, heading in the direction of Baltimore's Inner Harbor.

Hearses leaving the medical examiner's office were a common sight, although it was slightly unusual to see one departing at three o'clock in the morning.

Seconds after the hearse left, the garage gate in the basement of the medical examiner's building automatically slid closed, as it was programmed to.

The driver of the hearse never saw this, of course. By this point he was busily avoiding bumps and potholes in Baltimore's cratered downtown streets, lest he deliver a rough ride to his passenger. God knew that she had already been brutalized enough.

"Never stopped loving you, baby," her driver said. "Ain't loved nobody like that since." He glanced in the rearview mirror, halfway hoping to see her sitting in the backseat, miraculously restored to the way she was prior to April 22, 1984, a funny, vivacious thirty-five-year-old with the body of a twenty-one-year-old and luminous, mischievous eyes that set his innards ablaze.

And a voice that sounded like a goddess when she talked and like God's favorite angel when she sang.

But the only thing in the rearview mirror was a massive white body bag that looked almost empty. God was punishing him by letting him see her like this.

The gunman pulled off his stocking mask and ran a hairy hand through his soaked, wavy black hair. She'd loved to run her hands through his hair when they made love. Which wasn't often, because her possessive, suspicious fiancé was always lurking nearby.

It didn't take long for her final ride to end, and the hearse pulled into the driveway of Washington Funeral Home, located in West Baltimore. The gunman had taken a fifteen-minute jaunt that took him back nearly two decades, to some of the best memories of his life. He'd never met another woman who made him feel like she had.

He knew he never would, too, which was part of his punishment. He didn't *deserve* anyone remotely like her.

Before the hearse's wheels had a chance to stop turning, Hubert Washington opened the front door to his business and ran toward the vehicle, dressed in a white T-shirt, black dress slacks, black socks, and no shoes.

The balding, rotund funeral home owner skittered to the passenger side of the hearse, opened the front door, and flopped onto the passenger seat. His eyes were practically bulging with fear.

"Where is it?" he whispered, looking around as if Lucifer were hiding in the neatly trimmed shrubbery surrounding his funeral home.

Where is *it*? The gunman took instant offense. She wasn't some "it," some sack of waste to be disposed of. "If you mean

the young lady, she in the back," he said, glaring contemptuously at Washington.

"Everything I've ever accomplished in life is on the line
here," Washington whimpered. "Help me get it inside." He
ran to the back of the hearse and began yanking out the plastic body bag. However, he immediately stopped when a huge,
gloved hand roughly encircled his left wrist.

"I got it, Mr. Washington," the gunman said evenly. "Why
don't you g'wan inside and get everything prepared?"

"This shit is crazy, Gregory," Washington sputtered, sprint-
ing toward his front door. "Your brother is *fucking crazy*!"

As far as that last statement was concerned, the two men
were in total agreement.

Bending his knees slightly, Gregory scooped the body bag
into his arms. He could feel the outline of a bony hand
through the plastic, along with two knobby knees. Cradling
the bag in his arms, Gregory pushed the rear door of the
hearse closed with his shoulder and slowly walked into the
Washington Funeral Home's lobby.

His feet had barely crossed the threshold before Hubert
Washington was slamming the door shut, lest anyone spy
Gregory and his cargo. Although Washington had done nothing to exert himself, dark semicircles of perspiration were already forming on his undershirt, near his armpits.

Gregory noticed the sweat, which only intensified his
negative feelings for the fat grave digger.

"Follow me downstairs," Washington said, motioning
toward an unpainted wooden door leading to the funeral
home's basement. Lugging the body bag, Gregory obediently
followed Washington into a brightly lit room that looked like
a smaller version of the autopsy suites at the medical examiner's office.

Stainless-steel medical equipment was neatly arrayed

around the room, along with glass and plastic bottles filled with exotic-looking fluids. The air in the room was filled with sharp-smelling odors, primarily those of bleach, formaldehyde, and wood alcohol.

Stopping in front of a porcelain embalming table, Washington gestured for Gregory to lay the body down. "Take it out of the bag, please," he said agitatedly. Gregory noticed Washington's left eye twitching as though being zapped with 110 volts.

Sighing, Gregory unzipped the bag. A smell—a cross between musty basement and fresh vinegar—flew out of the bag, wrinkling Gregory's nose. Washington, however, seemed not to notice.

"You may want to wear gloves," Washington said, but Gregory ignored him. He wasn't dealing with some nasty, potentially contagious corpse. He was dealing with his lover.

A flood of positive remembrances swept over Gregory when he pulled off the body bag and caught sight of her signature bracelet, the one with white gold mounting and fifty-six princess-cut diamonds. He had worked so hard to purchase that thing.

Her hand had flown to her mouth and the tears of joy seemed as though they would never stop.

That was the first time Gregory had ever seen her cry—until the day she died, that is. Upon seeing her lifeless, nude body, the emotions of that horrible day erupted inside him anew.

Something else Gregory noticed was a long, hideous incision that went from her breastbone all the way to her navel. Must be the handiwork of those medical examiner people.

Using his bare hands, he lifted Adrienne's right arm slightly. It felt like a length of bone surrounded by strips of ultratough beef jerky. Gregory slipped the bracelet from her arm, a circular indentation marking the spot where it had remained for eighteen years. Gregory slipped the bracelet into the left pocket of his black leather overcoat as Washington watched.

When Gregory saw the gold-and-platinum engagement ring on her left hand, with its hideous two-karat round-cut diamond, Gregory's eyes narrowed. His *brother* had given that *thing* to her. Roughly prying apart her stiff fingers, Gregory rotated the ring so that the diamond was forever shielded from view.

"Is that who I think it is?" Washington asked triumphantly. In the course of watching Gregory handle the corpse and its jewelry, nervousness had given way to discovery, then astonishment. "After all these years?"

Reaching into the left pocket of his overcoat, Gregory yanked out a fat manila envelope. Smoothly pulling a switchblade from his pants pocket, he slowly sliced the envelope open in a menacing way, his beady eyes trained on Washington the entire time. The envelope held fifty crisp hundred-dollar bills that Gregory fanned across the porcelain embalming table as if they were playing cards.

"This all you need to think about. From my crazy brother."

"Help me get her into the retort," Washington said, remembering why Gregory was there in the first place.

"In the what?"

"The oven. Help me get her into the oven." Washington disappeared into the next room and reappeared with a cremation tray—an open cardboard box big enough to hold a human body, with sides about six inches high. The funeral director set the cremation tray on the red tile floor, next to the embalming table. Then Washington snapped on a pair of beige latex gloves.

"I got it," Gregory said simply. Her body had been locked into a fetal position for nearly two decades, so her legs and feet didn't fit cleanly inside the cremation tray. Gregory tried gently to force her within the confines of the box.

"It doesn't matter," Washington said softly, finally under-standing that the body they were dealing with was more than a mere corpse to Gregory. Washington was brimming with questions but restrained himself. Gregory had always been a hair-trigger sort, whereas his brother was calm, deliberate, and calculating. Not to mention much smarter.

Under ordinary circumstances, Washington would have needed a document from the deceased woman's family that authorized him to cremate her remains. But this was a crema-tion unlike any Washington had performed in all his years in the funeral business. He promised himself that he would never do another cremation like this one, either.

"Let's move next door."

With Washington easily picking up one end of the tray and Gregory the other, they carried the woman into an ad-joining room, where the Washington Funeral Home's crema-tory was located. The men set the dead woman's body in front of a blue metal machine seven feet tall, and about twice as long.

An ALL Model 2001 cremator, it weighed tons and was operated by using a push-button control panel.

Gregory noticed that Washington kept looking at the woman oddly.

"Uh, whatcha gonna do with her diamond ring?" Wash-ington asked sheepishly.

"Diamond carbon, ain't it?" Gregory barked. "Gonna burn that shit up."

Washington said nothing and started fiddling with the cremator's control panel. "If you're just going to burn it, can I, uh, have it?" he said, adjusting the cremator's controls with his back to Gregory.

"Yeah, whatever. Be my guest." *You blood-sucking bastard!*

Washington practically pounced in his eagerness to pry the engagement ring off her left hand. Gregory was sorely tempted to take out his gun and knock Washington cold, then have him join her in the flames.

The only reason he didn't was because he didn't know how to operate the ALL Model 2001 without Washington's help.

Once the ring was safely in one of Washington's chubby, latex-covered hands, he walked back to the control panel. He began pushing buttons then turned a knob. A three-foot brushed aluminum door yawned open. It exposed the interior of the ALL Model 2001, basically a glorified furnace made for burning human beings.

"Lift on three and we'll stick her inside," Washington commanded. "One, two three."

The cremation tray was gently shoved into the cremator. When Washington pushed a button closing the outer door, Gregory realized he'd taken his last earthly glimpse of her.

Trying to remain composed outwardly, he quickly flicked a tear from his right eye before Washington could see it.

"Can I watch?" Gregory said quietly.

"Sure," Washington said, preparing to light natural gas jets that would take about forty minutes to reduce her shriveled body to three pounds of gray ash. "The door has a little observation port."

A hum like an air conditioner's began to resonate within the room. It was the crematory's ventilation system, which had special filters to keep offending odors from wafting through the surrounding neighborhood.

As Gregory put his eye against the observation port, a muffled *pssssssssssst-whoomp!* could be heard through the door, the sound of the natural gas entering the ALL Model 2001 and igniting.

Huge jets of fire were directed right at the cremation tray, which was immediately transformed from an inanimate object into a squirming mass of yellow flames that danced crazily as they devoured the cardboard tray.

Gregory couldn't tell at what point the flames began feeding on the body. Her dry remains practically exploded like a discarded Christmas tree set ablaze.

The chemical compounds in her corpse occasionally sent spectacular tongues of red-and-green fire spiraling heavenward, convincing Gregory that he was watching her soul leave her body. Finally she was being liberated.

In no time, her skull and ribs were starting to show, the bones seeming to glow white from the intense flames. The bones of her hands stayed intact for quite some time, the ligaments binding them together defiantly resisting the fiery hurricane obliterating the rest of her body.

Eventually, though, like everyone else who had entered the ALL Model 2001 before her, the woman simply disintegrated. Pieces of her spine were still distinguishable, but that was about it.

"Do you want her remains?" Washington asked gently, relieved that evidence of his potentially career-ending crime had gone up in smoke.

Gregory answered by loping upstairs, hopping into his car, and screeching out of the Washington Funeral Home's parking lot.

"Both them brothers damned fools," Washington muttered, collecting his hundred-dollar bills from the embalming table and stacking them into two neat piles.

CHAPTER 10

Once they're safely at home, away from job-related tension and stress, cops hate to get an unexpected knock at the door. It could be some pimply-faced neighborhood kid, selling candy for a school fund-raising drive, or it could be a gun-toting psychopath still seething over a misdemeanor arrest that took place a decade ago.

"Damn!"

Decked out in a flame-red terry cloth robe, her right ear covered in gauze, homicide detective Thelma Holmes abandoned her cereal bowl and padded in her slippered feet toward her bedroom.

"Hold on; I'll be right there."

She had purchased her little out-of-the-way house on an acre and a half of heavily wooded land in West Baltimore

County expressly so she wouldn't be bothered by unexpected visitors. Her home was so far off the beaten path that anyone knocking on her door had to be looking for her.

And the last time she checked, her social calendar was empty. Just like she wanted it, in light of the jarring events of the previous day. Standing on tiptoe, Thelma ran one hand along the dusty top shelf of her closet, feeling for the Magnum Research Desert Eagle .357 resting there. As she felt the cold steel against her right hand, Thelma fished the key for the semiautomatic pistol's gun lock out of her left robe pocket.

Tired, depressed, and ornery after seeing three people shot and killing a teenage boy herself, Thelma was in no mood for trifles. Whoever was at her front door had better state their business quickly and be done with it.

Keeping a finger firmly on the trigger of her large handgun, which she slid into the right pocket of her robe, Thelma stood just to the right of her door, instead of looking through the peephole. "Who's there?" she barked in an unmistakable cop's command voice.

"Darryl Billups, with the *Baltimore Herald*," came the quick reply.

"I don't *read* the *Herald*," Thelma shot back. "Go away!"

"Scott Donatelli is a friend of mine."

Meant to get on Thelma Holmes's good side, Darryl's name-dropping only pissed her off further. She hadn't forgotten her relentless hazing at Donatelli's hands—yesterday hadn't erased all that. So a friend of Donatelli's wasn't automatically a buddy of hers.

Relaxing her grip on the handgun, Thelma released both dead bolts from the door and cracked it a couple of inches. Standing close to the screen was a trim, somewhat muscular black man of medium height who had a strong chin, handsome nose, hairline on the verge of scraping his eyebrows, and soft-looking, kissable lips. And he had one of those ultrathin Clark Gable playboy mustaches that Thelma couldn't stand.

"Hi, my name is Darryl Billups. I'm a reporter—"

"I know who you are." Thelma had seen him in the newspaper and on television enough times to know exactly who he was. And she was unimpressed.

"How did you find my house?"

Darryl's eyebrows rose to meet his hairline. He had already formed a mental picture of what this lady cop would look like, and Detective Thelma Jones far surpassed his meager expectations. Even though the door was barely cracked, Darryl could see that she was quite attractive, despite the gauze earring she wore.

"I got your address from someone at police headquarters," Darryl lied. Actually, he'd gotten it from Donatelli.

"Let me see some ID."

Thelma cracked the door a tad wider to snatch Darryl's press pass. He noticed that her right hand stayed in the pocket of her well-proportioned robe and observed the outline of her .357 Magnum.

You happy to see me, hon? Or is that a gun?

While that silly thought rattled through Darryl's brain, Thelma casually tossed the press pass back in his general direction. It fluttered down to her wooden front porch, striking Darryl's right shoe.

"Listen, pal, I'm off duty," Thelma said wearily. "Don't you *ever* come out here again, understand?"

Clearly oblivious to the fact that he was on the verge of getting cuffed and read his rights for trespassing, Darryl continued to press forward.

"I didn't mean to disturb you," he said gravely. "Just a couple of questions and I'll be out of your hair."

Thelma Holmes finally removed her right hand from her robe pocket—to shut the door in Darryl Billups's face. "Call the PIO!" she yelled.

Hhmmmpppphh! Only inexperienced or lazy reporters relied on the police department's public information officer. Darryl, whose writing and reporting had been nominated for a Pulitzer Prize on two occasions, had no intention of letting the police spoon-feed him what they wanted him to know.

"The Safe&Sound body is missing—did you know that?" he yelled back through the door.

Already halfway back to the kitchen and her now soggy bowl of cereal, Thelma stopped in midstride. "What did you say?" she cried.

"Open the door," Darryl said quietly, making his voice barely audible. "I'll tell you what I know."

Thelma pulled her robe tightly around her and opened the front door a little wider this time. But she locked the screen door and once again wrapped her hand around the huge, comforting handgun.

"Go ahead," she said with an impatient wave. "What do you know?"

"Only that the woman's body was taken to the medical examiner's and somebody stole it this morning."

Beneath her deadpan expression, Thelma couldn't believe what she was hearing. She had gotten shot because of this body, as had Donatelli, Joseph Dennis, Adele Jones, and that sixteen-year-old. And now someone had casually nabbed the corpse at the center of all the mayhem!

Thelma literally felt nauseous. "How do you know all this?" she demanded.

Darryl responded by withdrawing his notebook from his rear pocket. A ballpoint pen magically appeared in his right hand. "If you let me in for a minute, I'll tell you." He was un-smiling, determined, and all business. But so was Thelma.

"That's not necessary," she said coolly. "I'm just curious how you found that out."

Darryl snapped his notebook shut and shoved it back in his pocket. He had a lot of stops to make and this one was rapidly going nowhere. "My sources," he said simply.

"Look, I'm on administrative leave, as you probably know," Thelma said, starting to push the door shut again. "I can't talk about this case—good-bye!"

Thelma slid both heavy dead bolts back into place, then watched from her living room window to make sure Darryl drove off. Once he was under way, trailing a cloud of tan dust down the dirt-covered road leading to her house, she stalked disgustedly back toward her bedroom, put the gun lock back in her revolver, and placed the weapon back in the closet.

In law enforcement, there are times when all the dedication and good intentions in the world don't seem to amount to a hill of beans because there just seems to be too much crime and too many dirtbags. This was one of those moments for Thelma.

Feeling fatigued and queasy—and certain the S&S body had disappeared, just as Darryl said—she plopped back into bed, pulled her satin sheets up to her chin, and drifted off to sleep.

Meanwhile, Darryl motored along in the direction of Baltimore City, turning over the facets of the S&S case in his head. Who was the dead woman at the center of this case?

She had to be someone incredibly important, Darryl reasoned. Why else would so many people get shot because of her? Then there was the awesome-looking diamond-studded bracelet she wore, in addition to the huge rock on her finger.

Poor folks didn't wear jewelry like that, so this woman either was someone of means or had an affluent lover. Somebody who wore that kind of jewelry and abruptly vanished had to be missed by somebody.

Darryl had a hunch that Lady S&S was probably from the Baltimore area and that someone had filed a missing person report on her. Chances were that her description made mention of her gaudy bracelet and ring. When Darryl stopped by the *Herald*, he planned to visit the paper's library and look up old missing persons stories from the 1980s.

The dead woman's bracelet and ring told Darryl something else, too: Her death probably stemmed from a crime of passion. If mere robbery were the motive, why would her killer leave behind such expensive jewelry?

This case has a ton of secrets and mysteries running through it, Darryl thought contentedly. In *seven* years of working at the *Baltimore Herald*, for example, he had never heard of someone pilfering a body from the custody of the medical examiner's office.

For a stiff to disappear like that meant that the theft was probably an inside job. Thanks to a previous story involving the ME's office, Darryl already had a short list of officials who could grant access to the basement of the medical examiner's building.

The head of the Maryland State Police was one, as well as the chief of pathology for the University of Maryland Medical School and Baltimore's health commissioner. Oh yes, there was also Chief Medical Examiner Dr. Harold Roth and about thirty or so assistant medical examiners working under him.

Darryl scratched Roth off the list. Who in his right mind would want to have the corpse at the center of a high-profile murder case vanish during his watch?

The top cop for the state police was the first African-American to hold the position and such an eager-to-please Negro that Darryl quickly ruled him out, too.

Darryl didn't know the chief pathologist at the University of Maryland Medical School, nor had he ever met the city's health commissioner. He needed to start collecting string on all of them as soon as possible. First, though, Darryl began to drive in the direction of the medical examiner's building, to see if it had a video monitoring system.

He parked around the corner from the building's front entrance, in a parking lot that was near the ramp used by hearses and vans to ferry bodies in and out of the basement.

It was an overcast, hot and humid Sunday and ordinarily would have been Darryl's day off. At the moment, however, he was professionally obligated to be working on the Safe&Sound story. Anyway, the alternative was to amble into St. Peter Claver Church, where he hadn't been seen in weeks, then return home and think about Yolanda and Jamal all day.

A local television crew was working in front of the medical examiner's building when Darryl arrived, the towering white microwave antenna of their van almost as tall as the three-story ME's building.

Darryl walked past the reporter unnoticed. She was too busy flubbing the opening lines to her piece over and over again to notice as Darryl moved toward the glass double doors leading into the building.

Standing just inside the lobby was a fierce-looking female Maryland state trooper.

"I'd like to talk to the medical examiner, please," Darryl said, taking his press pass from his wallet for the second time that morning. The trooper subjected it to such exaggerated scrutiny that Darryl felt vaguely insulted. One might have thought Darryl was the prime suspect in the Safe&Sound body snatching, the way the trooper squinted and frowned while examining his credential. Finally satisfied that Darryl was the person he claimed to be, she handed his press pass back to him. "I'll be right back, sir," she said brusquely.

The trooper walked off, leaving Darryl standing unsupervised in the lobby. If he were a bad guy, it would be a simple matter for him to walk into a nearby stairwell and disappear.

Darryl turned and looked up, in case a video camera was near the ceiling. As he did so, the female trooper returned and she shot him a curious look.

"Dr. Roth says it's okay for you to come back to his office," she said, pointing down a hallway to the second door on the left. That pleasantly surprised Darryl, who was expecting to have to deal with one of Dr. Roth's minions.

The medical examiner worked in a richly appointed oak-paneled office that looked like it was inside a white-shoe law firm, instead of a government building.

Whenever he was about to interview someone he'd never met, Darryl liked to play a game of imagining what the person would look like. He had figured Dr. Roth would be in his late fifties and wearing a neatly trimmed salt-and-pepper beard. Instead, the chief medical examiner appeared to be in his late thirties and was clean-shaven.

On the wall hung a diploma from Northwestern Medical School, as well as one from Temple University. The only artwork in the office was a crudely drawn crayon picture showing a masked doctor operating on a nude patient. Darryl guessed the patient was dead, based on the fact that Xs had been substituted for eyes.

Leaning against the wall near the doorway leading to Roth's office were a pair of aluminum crutches. Probably explaining why he failed to rise when Darryl entered his office.

"Please excuse me," Roth said, a sheepish expression on his face, "but I blew out my Achilles playing basketball." He extended his hand and Darryl walked over to shake it. The doctor had a surprisingly forceful grip. "Have a seat," he said, motioning Darryl toward a chair in front of his desk. "Coffee, soft drink?"

Darryl shook his head.

"I guess you're wondering how we could lose a body, huh?" Dr. Roth said, cutting to the chase. "Well, I'm holding a news conference in about two hours to explain everything," he added without waiting for Darryl's response.

"I'm not here to deal with that, actually," Darryl said, laying his tape recorder on Dr. Roth's desk. "Another *Herald* reporter will be at the press conference. I came to see you to find out if there's a video system in the building."

"You mean downstairs, where the bodies are?"

Darryl nodded.

"You mean a monitoring system, right?"

"Yes."

"No, actually, there isn't. We have a number of safe-guards, documentation and what have you, that have always been more than adequate in the past. We're not in the habit of losing bodies here," Dr. Roth said a tad defensively.

"Because generally speaking, dead people don't walk off," Dr. Roth continued. "And there hasn't been a body snatching in Baltimore since the eighteen-hundreds, when medical schools in need of cadavers were in the habit of misappropri-ating corpses."

"Could one of your employees be involved in the disap-pearance of the Safe&Sound woman?"

Darryl expected an indignant, snap response, but Dr. Roth stroked his chin thoughtfully instead. "No," he replied firmly. "No one on my staff is involved in this—you can quote me on that. As bad as this situation is, we haven't reached that point."

Darryl asked for permission to go downstairs and view the autopsy suites, along with the intake refrigerator from which the body had disappeared. That would enable him to add valuable descriptive details to the story he had to write.

Dr. Roth shrugged. "No harm in that, I guess."

An autopsy assistant accompanied Darryl to the basement, bird-dogging his every step. Darryl was surprised to encounter homicide detective Lt. Tuck Anders in the basement, along with another detective. As had been the case at the Safe&Sound, Anders was in no mood to talk to Darryl.

Before brushing Darryl off, though, he did call the missing body "the damnedest thing I ever saw." Darryl scribbled down that quote.

Oddly, the area around the autopsy suites smelled like a hospital, catching Darryl by surprise, because he didn't associate the odor of disinfectant with dead people. But the medical examiner's basement needed to be disinfected and cleaned as regularly as a hospital, if not more so. Corpses brought with them a steady stream of infectious agents, including the viruses that cause AIDS and hepatitis B.

After taking a good look around, Darryl was escorted back upstairs and out of the building by the autopsy assistant. Darryl gave the man one of his *Baltimore Herald* business cards just in case but guessed the card would be in the trash can before Darryl reached the parking lot.

His next stop was one he definitely dreaded—a call to the family of shooting victim Alonzo Ellis, who lived in West Baltimore. Although Darryl didn't want to go, it would be helpful to have some background on a sixteen-year-old who wound up firing shots at city cops.

Darryl was surprised to encounter a fine, misty rain when he left the medical examiner's building. There had been a few scattered clouds in the sky when he entered the building, but it certainly hadn't appeared that rain was right around the corner.

Tucking his reporter's notebook into his back pocket to shield it from the moisture, Darryl walked to his car immersed in thought.

He was so preoccupied that he didn't notice the left

rear tire was flat until he opened the door to his vehicle. No problem—that's why he kept an aerosol can of flat fixer in his trunk.

But as Darryl went to open the trunk, he noticed that the left front tire was also flat.

Darryl spun around to see if anyone was watching him. But the parking lot was empty, save for one other car that had no one in it.

"Damn!"

Already having a good idea of what his search would yield, Darryl slowly walked around his coupe. All four tires were flatter than week-old beer, damaged by someone who'd methodically sliced the valve stem on each tire. "Shit!"

Who would possibly stoop to slashing tires on a Sunday morning? . . . Yolanda!

Steaming, Darryl sat inside his incapacitated vehicle to get out of the rain. Whenever a male friend related how his car had been scratched or otherwise damaged by a vengeful female, Darryl had always laughed uproariously. But there was nothing vaguely humorous about this situation.

Angrily snatching his cell phone from his briefcase, Darryl punched in the numbers 411.

"Can I have the Baltimore, Maryland, phone number for LaToya Winslow, please?"

"I'll connect you, sir."

LaToya's phone began to ring as Darryl glanced at his watch. It was almost eleven-thirty, so she, Yolanda, and Jamal might be in church.

"Hello."

"Hey, LaToya," Darryl said, straining not to sound peeved. "How've you been?"

His answer was a lengthy moment of silence, then a tone three times colder than Christmas in Minneapolis.

"Look, she doesn't want to talk, okay? Please leave us alone."

"I'm not dying to talk to her, either," Darryl said emphatically. "But this is important."

Another moment of hostile silence followed. Growing more impatient by the second, Darryl watched as little flecks of mist accumulated on his windshield, then formed streaks of moisture that ran down the shatterproof glass.

When Darryl was a boy, his temper was so explosive that it occasionally scared even him.

After each outburst, his mother would always caution, "Darryl, those who you let make you angry control you." He thought of those wise words while waiting for LaToya's response.

"Hold on!" she finally hissed, sounding disgusted.

After what seemed like twenty minutes, Yolanda picked up the phone. "Hey, Darryl," she said in an upbeat way. The old Yolanda, the sweet human being capable of loving and being loved. Not the she-devil of recent months. "What's up?"

"You don't know?" Darryl shot back. "I'm sitting here in downtown Baltimore in a car with four flat tires!"

"And you think *I had something to do with that*?" On the heels of LaToya's cold shoulder, now fiery indignation scorched through Darryl's little black cell phone. "This why we ain't together now, dumb ass—you don't even know me." *Click.*

Darryl calmly jabbed a button on his phone to terminate the call. Being a bottom-line kind of person, he began to assess his situation. The bottom line was that he had a story to pursue and he needed transportation to do it. As infuriating as his predicament was, he would have to worry about finding the guilty party later.

Rather than trek ten blocks in the rain to the *Baltimore*

Herald, which would waste even more time, Darryl called the *Herald* and arranged to be picked up. Then he called a towing company to fetch his vehicle from the medical examiner's parking lot.

Something or someone was trying to deter Darryl, to frustrate him.

CHAPTER 11

"Gregory! My man!"

Despite the cheery greeting, the man who worked in the oak-paneled office nearly defecated on himself upon seeing his brother at the front door. They were handling business that shouldn't be discussed in a man's home, not around unsuspecting family members.

What had prompted this visit to the older brother's ugly white-and-brown two-story Tudor on a Sunday morning? Plus why was baby brother dressed head-to-toe in black, wearing a full-length leather overcoat in the middle of August, and looking surly and implacable?

"Gonna lemme in?" Gregory grunted.

"My man, my man," the elder sibling said soothingly, holding on to his phony grin. "Why don't we go for a little ride?" He glanced over his shoulder at his pretty wife, who was puttering around in the kitchen, then turned back around and mouthed the word "please."

"Been riding around all night and all morning, taking care of *our* business," Gregory said stubbornly. "I'm tired—lemme in."

"Sweetie, who's at the door?" Gloria Hudson came bounding out of the kitchen, looking like a million dollars. Gregory never could understand how his miserable sibling consistently attracted decent, pretty women. Women willing to baby him and cater to him and turn a blind eye to his incessant philandering.

Even now, fifteen years into her marriage, Gloria continued to rise an hour before her disgusting husband, so that she could put her "face" on before he got out of bed.

"Gregory!" she squealed, delighted to see him. "Come on in here, you handsome devil. Had breakfast?"

Gregory looked at his brother and smirked. From time to time Gregory toyed with the idea of seducing Gloria, just to get back at his sibling. The twisted rivalry that linked and repelled the brothers would probably end only after one of them died.

"Naw, Glo, I ain't ate yet," Gregory said amiably. His sister-in-law waltzed over to him and planted a big lipstick print on his right cheek. Her makeup was impeccable, as always. She was a sweet, spectacular woman who shouldn't be sharing her man with some big-titty bimbo, unbeknownst to her. Frowning disgustedly, Gregory shook his head.

"What's wrong, Greg?" Gloria asked, taking his black leather overcoat and hanging it in the closet. She never thought to ask why he was wearing a Darth Vader getup in the middle of summer. "You okay, baby?"

Gregory laughed. "You so fine, every time I see you I just shake my head. What do you see in my brother?"

"Oh, Greg, stop," Gloria laughed, ignoring her husband's

disapproving glare. "Come on in here and get some breakfast, boy!"

"Thank you, baby girl. You a sweetie." Predictably, Gloria beamed, before excusing herself to the bathroom.

"Come here, Bro'," a grim-faced Gregory said as soon as Gloria left the room. When that command was ignored, Gregory sauntered over to his big brother, who was still standing by the front door as if trying to will Gregory back outside.

Grabbing his sibling's shoulder with a viselike right hand, Gregory rubbed his other hand on his brother's face. "What's that smell like, Bro'?" he asked in a taunting voice.

"Vinegar—so what? Why the hell did you come here?"

"Not vinegar," Gregory said in a low, conspiratorial voice, looking down at his brother, who was three inches shorter. "That's Adrienne—nice odor, huh?"

Charles Hudson didn't move for several seconds because the horrible reality of what Gregory had done took a while to register. When it did, Charles flew toward the basement bathroom, sputtering and cursing while he lathered and rinsed his face several times to get rid of the offending odor.

Then he sprinted into the kitchen. Gregory and Gloria were seated at the kitchen table, laughing as bacon sizzled behind them on the stove. Their body language looked suspiciously intimate.

"Why did you do that?" Charles demanded, nostrils flaring. Gregory and Gloria both stopped midsentence and turned to stare quizzically at Charles.

"What are you talking about, honey?" Gloria asked, genuinely alarmed.

"Yeah, what are you talking about, hon?" Gregory asked with a knowing grin. "You okay, man?"

Gloria got up, fetched a fork, and began expertly flipping the bacon. "Stop fooling around, you guys. Come join us, sweetie. Breakfast is almost ready."

"I'm not hungry," Charles Hudson said forcefully, sitting at the kitchen table without speaking another word. Gloria was so accustomed to the weird dynamic between her husband and brother-in-law that she paid them no heed.

They made an odd breakfast threesome; sullen Charles Hudson, who sat mutely and didn't eat, and Gregory Hudson and Gloria Hudson, who casually chatted and laughed as though no one else were present.

Gregory and Gloria chatted and laughed for about fifteen minutes before Gloria noticed that her husband was staring intently at Gregory, who had a piece of toast in one hand and a butter knife in the other.

"What's wrong, baby?" Gloria asked, laughing.

But Charles Hudson didn't smile. "Hey, Greg," he said in a low voice, "aren't you going to *wash* your hands?"

Greg slowly laid his toast on his plate, on top of his scrambled eggs and bacon. He brought his right hand to his face and sniffed at it, then rubbed it across his mustache. "I'm cool," Gregory said defiantly. "What's wrong?"

Then Gregory patted Gloria on the back, as if comforting her, and made a point of enclosing one of her dainty café au lait hands inside both of his beefy brown ones. Ensuring that Adrienne's molecules and scent would finally meet Gloria's, if only from beyond the grave.

Charles grimaced, to Gregory's delight.

"What in the world is up with you guys?" Gloria asked, sensing that the two men at her kitchen table might be close to trading blows.

"If you only knew," Gregory muttered darkly. "If you only knew."

Neither brother said much of anything after that, each choosing instead to stare darkly at the other.

"Your food is getting cold, Greg," Gloria said quietly, suddenly fearful of the unpredictable Hudson men. With her appetite diminished because of all the negativity and weirdness in the air, Gloria abruptly got up from the table. "I'm going to take a bath."

Charles's and Gregory's eyes remained locked in combat.

"How dare you?" Charles growled. "Don't you ever come here again, understand?"

Gregory merely yawned. Brains and intellectuality were Charles's domain. But when it came to physicality, Charles only amused Gregory. Even though Gregory was the younger brother, he had always been able to run faster and jump higher. Not to mention whipping Charles's ass at will.

"You don't care about Gloria," Gregory said, studying his now cold piece of toast. Feeling a belch building in his gullet, Gregory released it and blew it in his brother's face.

"You disgusting piece of shit—get out!" Charles shouted, leaping to his feet.

Gregory calmly wiped his lips with a napkin and gracefully lifted his six-foot-four prizefighter's frame from his chair. He looked down at his shorter brother and chuckled. "Who's gonna make me leave—you?" Laughing harder now, he walked to the hall closet near the front door and removed his full-length black leather coat. He draped it around his shoulders slowly and regally, a king donning his cape.

Water continued to run upstairs, meaning Gloria was drawing her bath and couldn't hear a thing. That was Gregory's cue to walk back over to where Charles stood, to the point of their being nearly nose-to-nose.

"Who's gonna make me leave, punk?"

"Want to punch me around, Greg? If it makes you feel better, swing away," Charles sneered. "You're still the same two-bit thug you were back in high school. I've tried to make something of my life since our mistake, but you—"

His soliloquy was cut short by a brutal roundhouse right hand, exploding beneath his left eye. Charles staggered back

but somehow remained upright. Less fortunate were his tor-
toiseshell reading glasses, which soared across the room before crashing to the floor, broken in half.

"Can't outrun your past, motherfucka," Gregory said.
"You can run, but you sure as hell can't hide. Little Bro' may
see to that himself."

With that, Gregory Hudson turned up the collar of his
coat and walked out the door into the misting rain.

IN A PART OF BALTIMORE far removed from Charles
Hudson's tony Roland Park neighborhood, Darryl Billups
steeled himself for something journalists truly loathe and do
frequently—interviewing the survivors of accident victims.

Darryl had just rung Alonzo Ellis's doorbell, the teenage
shooter capped at the Safe&Sound. As was his custom, Darryl
half-hoped no one would answer.

The rain had stopped, leaving a gorgeous, sunshine-filled
midsummer day in its wake. Darryl was just about to scamper
away from the porch of Alonzo Ellis's row house on Edmond-
son Avenue in West Baltimore when the door eased open, revealing a pudgy black youth about twelve years old. He wore
an extra-large Baltimore Ravens jersey with a purple 52 on it,
the number of All-Pro linebacker Ray Lewis.

"Who you is?" he said suspiciously, eyeing Darryl's reporter's notebook and conservative work attire.

"I'm a reporter with the *Baltimore Herald*," Darryl said
softly.

"Daddy! Some reporter wants to know about Alonzo."

A plainly dressed man roughly Darryl's age quickly came
to the door and gently pushed his roly-poly son to the side.
The man's eyes were red and surrounded by dark circles, and
his breath smelled of alcohol.

Looking at the man's ashy, callused hands, Darryl surmised that he was a manual laborer. To Darryl's relief, the man smiled warmly and extended a hand. Survivors sometimes have to be cajoled into talking and every now and then are downright hostile. But that didn't appear to be the case this time.

"Stanley Ellis is the name," the wiry man said wearily. "You're the first reporter that bothered to talk to us, to get our side. Come on in."

Darryl followed Stanley Ellis into his neat, modestly furnished home smelling of freshly baked rolls. It was a wonderful aroma Darryl remembered well from summers spent at his grandmama's house in southern Maryland.

Stanley Ellis showed Darryl to a threadbare blue sofa. Sitting down, Darryl realized he was beat! How nice it would be to get horizontal on Stanley Ellis's sofa and take an hour-long nap.

"Offer you sumthin'? Beer, water?"

Darryl politely declined and Ellis launched into his spiel. "I can't tell you how to write your story," he began, "but you tell people that Alonzo is . . . was . . . a good boy." Ellis's eyes began to tear up, but his voice remained strong and he didn't stop talking. "You tell people his parents love him and did right by him. A lot of folks in this city think all black males is hoodlums with parents that don't care. Well, my Alonzo wasn't no hoodlum. He wasn't no angel, neither, but he damn sure wasn't no cop shooter."

Seeing that Stanley Ellis was on a roll, Darryl nudged his tape recorder closer to Ellis and let the man unburden. Good reporters know when to shut up and let a source carry the day. But when Ellis launched into a rambling, emotional rant about police brutality, Darryl gently interrupted.

"Mr. Ellis, did your son have a gun?"

"No! Alonzo stole a couple o' cars and I got him out of jail for shoplifting. But he wasn't no shooter."

Darryl nodded, more to placate Ellis than out of agreement. He had interviewed parents of suspected murderers plenty of times, and only a handful acknowledged the possibility their child *might* be guilty. The rest were certain little Johnny or Raheem had been framed.

"Mr. Ellis, let me put it this way: If Alonzo *could* get a gun, and I'm not saying that he did, who would he get it from?"

Stanley Ellis looked at Darryl sharply. "You know, there's a toy gangster in the neighborhood named Mr. Greg," he responded after a few seconds. "He always up to no good, mostly minor shit. Nickel-and-dime reefer, stuff like that. Somebody said he talked to Alonzo once, but I ain't never seen no evidence o' that."

"Where could I find this Mr. Greg?"

Mr. Ellis looked Darryl up and down as if taking his measure. "In the Kit-Kat Club on Orleans Street, not far from Johns Hopkins Hospital. His brother is a bigwig with the city."

Darryl nearly toppled off the sofa—Mr. Greg's brother might have connections that could make a body vanish from the medical examiner's office. "What's Mr. Greg's last name?"

"Dunno. But if you go there, everybody know him," Mr. Ellis said, looking heartbroken. "Like I said, ain't no proof he knew Alonzo, though."

Darryl wrapped up the interview, thanked Mr. Ellis, and clasped the grieving man's hand. Even though Darryl wasn't a parent, he could empathize with having to bury a child. Baltimore was experiencing an epidemic of that.

Darryl made three other stops related to the Safe&Sound story before heading to the *Herald*, where he wrote a piece focusing on security lapses at the medical examiner's office.

The story was accompanied by a short piece highlighting the short, tragic life of Alonzo Ellis. Darryl knew that certain factions within the *Herald*'s editorial department would probably label him a "bleeding heart" and secretly castigate him for writing a story about Ellis instead of one of the victims. Not that Darryl gave a shit—writing about the teenager had nothing to do with liberalism and everything to do with good journalism. Aside from the mystery lady, whose corpse was found in Unit 25, Alonzo Ellis was the most fascinating player involved in the Safe&Sound case, in Darryl's estimation. Tomorrow's paper needed some indication of why a sixteen-year-old with no felony record had fallen to the depths of shooting at cops from a rooftop.

That would tick off a small group of *Herald* reporters who felt a liberal conspiracy was afoot to accentuate the rights of criminals, rather than victims. Personally, Darryl was disgusted by journalists who brought personal agendas to the table, whether righty or lefty. He had only one burning agenda, and that was to learn everything he could about Lady S&S. Including her age, birthplace, profession, shoe size—even whom she had sex with and how often. After learning every detail of this woman's life, Darryl planned to bring her back to life in the pages of the *Herald*.

Preferably before the cops found out the same details. Like most journalists, Darryl was highly competitive and loved the idea that when cops read his stories they might blurt, "Damn—how'd he find that out?"

Finished with his writing duties around seven o'clock, Darryl decided his best bet was to go home and get some sleep, then rise early tomorrow morning and do some research in the *Herald*'s library. So he left the newspaper and drove home, scaring himself silly by nearly falling asleep twice during the short trip. When Darryl made the sharp, downhill turn leading to his street, he spied several fire trucks blocking the way, their red lights flashing furiously. Although he was still two blocks away, Darryl noticed the commotion was on his side of the street.

A queasy sensation gripped his belly—the fire trucks were

gathered in front of *his* small house from which plumes of light-colored smoke blossomed and floated into the dark evening sky.

As Darryl drew nearer, he saw four fire trucks directing torrents of water inside his home.

Darryl slammed the brakes on his company car, jumped out, and began to dash over the bulging fire hoses draped along his lawn like strings of beige spaghetti.

From somewhere deep inside Darryl's house came a muffled explosion, then the sound of glass breaking. Probably an aerosol can.

The firefighters appeared bored because the fire wasn't much by their standards. But from Darryl's standpoint, they were battling the Great Chicago Fire of 1906. "What happened?" he asked, frantically grabbing the elbow of a helmeted firefighter trudging out the front door.

"Looks like the place was cocktailed." The fireman shrugged. "As in Molotov cocktail. Guess somebody doesn't like the owner."

Knowledge that the blaze may not have been accidental made the whole deal even more sickening and disheartening. Unable to watch any longer, he walked away from his place and back toward the street in a daze.

Sitting down at the curb, he cradled his head in his hands while a river of dirty water trickled under his legs. *Just a bad dream, kid. Close your eyes for three seconds, open then and you'll be lying in bed.*

When Darryl opened his eyes, smoke was still frantically cascading from his home. He lay his head in his hands, deciding not to watch. A fire captain came sloshing through a lawn now filled with mud instead of neatly trimmed grass land tapped Darryl's shoulder.

"You the owner?"

Darryl nodded.

"The living room is pretty well gone, but the fire didn't get much else. Lot of smoke and water damage, though. Sorry, pal."

The billowing smoke had turned nearly white now, instead of the brown Darryl had observed when he first pulled up. Spotting a man in a Baltimore City Arson Squad fire coat standing on the front steps, Darryl popped up and sprinted in his direction, dark brown mud splattering his shoes.

Arson investigator Ken Dyson was scribbling something in a notepad as Darryl approached.

"This is my house," Darryl said plaintively. "Any idea what started this?"

"Gasoline bomb," murmured Dyson, a frail-looking bearded man who practically disappeared inside his massive Baltimore City Arson Squad fire coat. "No doubt about it. Gas bomb."

Tempted to ask how Dyson was so certain, Darryl didn't bother. He was already suffering from information overload as it was.

Darryl also refused to yield to another temptation— assuming that Yolanda was behind all this. She could be moody and streety, but she wasn't evil enough to do something like this . . . was she?? If Dyson or the police asked for potential suspects, would Darryl mention Yolanda?

At the moment, he wasn't sure.

No longer wishing to see Dyson or anything else associated with his smoldering property, Darryl took one of Dyson's business cards and returned to his car, which had BALTIMORE HERALD emblazoned on both sides.

Spending the night with his parents was out of the question because his mother would freak out when she heard what had happened. And Darryl wasn't speaking to Camille. Mad Dawg would probably be noisily fornicating like a rabbit and smoking ganja until the wee hours of the morning.

So Darryl made a twenty-minute drive to Catonsville, a

working-class suburb not that far from his home. He had no problem staying awake this time—seeing his home burning was akin to downing three cups of coffee.

Using a company credit card, Darryl booked a room at a modest motel. He asked the night clerk to wake him up at 5:30, because he had to buy a toothbrush and a razor. He would worry about clothes later in the day.

After taking an extra-long hot shower in a bid to calm down, Darryl crawled into bed and turned off the light beside his bed. He closed his eyes but couldn't erase the mental image of his house burning. Furthermore, the motel room was filled with the smoky odor of Darryl's clothes, which he'd piled in front of the door to his room in case someone tried to enter.

When sleep finally made it Darryl's way, mercifully no dreams came with it.

CHAPTER 12

Baltimore homicide detective Scott Donatelli winced and gulped, in agony from the simple act of tying his shoe. Couldn't he do any fucking thing that didn't cause the muscles and cartilage around his injured rib to explode in pain?

So he remained hunched over in the men's locker room at police headquarters. His left shoe was already tied, but Donatelli was afraid to pivot toward his right shoe, whose loose laces dangled to the floor.

Earlier he had argued heatedly with a police doctor who didn't want to clear Donatelli to work. It had taken a comical display of jumping jacks and toe touching to convince that damn quack that Donatelli was physically fit to work.

As soon as he had a precious slip of paper with the doc's signature, Donatelli nearly collapsed in pain outside the physician's office.

But it would take a herd of oxen to keep him away from work this cloudless Monday morning. Initially the Safe&Sound storage facility case had just been Donatelli's job, but it had become a lot more than that.

That was definitely the case for Thelma Holmes, who was also back at work sporting a flesh-colored bandage that hid the chunk of flesh a .22-caliber bullet had blasted out of her right ear.

The police department had looked into her fatal shooting of sixteen-year-old Alonzo Ellis and found the shooting was justifiable. That surprised no one, given the facts of the case. Anyway, it was exceedingly rare for a black male's death at the hands of a city cop to be deemed unjustified.

As pretty as Thelma Holmes was, she was a bulldog, Donatelli came to realize belatedly. She was the real deal, a cop's cop, not the boy toy of some lecherous police captain or major.

The glint in Holmes's eye that morning made Donatelli appreciate how badly he'd misjudged her. That look told him two things—she badly wanted the person who'd deposited a dead woman's body at the Safe&Sound and she was still angry at Donatelli for treating her like a greenhorn.

That last didn't worry Donatelli too much—if she could channel her anger in a way that helped her do her job better, more power to her.

At the moment, Donatelli was more concerned with pain management than his relationship with his partner. He'd gulped three aspirin and, aside from making his stomach hurt, they weren't doing much to quiet the roaring volcano of pain in his side. As much as he wanted—needed—to hit the streets, Donatelli wouldn't be much good if he continued to hurt like this.

"You awright, Scott?"

Sensing a pair of eyes on him, Donatelli tried to straighten up and act nonchalant, as if nothing were bothering him. He almost pulled it off, too, sitting up in a smooth, easy motion. But his constipated expression drew the attention of his boss, Homicide Lieutenant Tuck Anders. The last person Donatelli wanted to see at the moment.

"I'm good to go, El Tee," Donatelli half grunted. He hoped Anders would go away soon, because it actually hurt to talk.

"Scott, I'm not looking for heroes, okay? I want people who can close this Safe&Sound deal," Anders said matter-of-factly. "If that ain't you today, say so and I'll call someone in to replace you."

"I'm good; I'm good," Donatelli said quickly, standing erect without bothering to tie his right shoe.

"Fine. Look, how are you and Thelma Holmes doing?"

"She's a helluva detective, El Tee. She saved my bacon out there the other day."

Anders nodded. Within a profession whose practitioners are sometimes called pigs, "saving someone's bacon" was the highest praise one Baltimore cop could give another.

"Scott, Thelma doesn't want to work with you anymore," Anders said with characteristic bluntness. "She wants to work with someone else once the Safe&Sound deal is closed."

Donatelli simply stared at his boss, dumbfounded. "Did she say why?"

Anders responded with a piercing look that seemed vaguely accusatory. "No, didn't get into details. Just said it would probably be in everyone's best interest."

Donatelli mentally reviewed his relationship with Holmes. He had been tough on her, sure. But no tougher than his mentor, Phil Gardner, had been on him.

"Okay, El Tee. Thanks for the heads-up."

Anders grinned lecherously. "Not trying to play 'hide the salami,' are we, Scott?" Anders shot Donatelli a burlesque wink before ambling out of the men's locker room to deal with other matters.

Donatelli slowly sat down on the bench again, easing his behind gingerly onto the unyielding wooden slab, lest he jar his tender rib cage. As he was a rising star in the homicide department, the last thing Donatelli needed was a hint of impropriety or scandal. Grunting in pain as he bent over to finally tie his right shoe, he weighed the best way to deal with Holmes.

Why should he have to bend over to kiss her ass or run like hell in the opposite direction? *She* was the newbie, not him. *She* should be the one walking on eggshells.

Holmes was waiting for Donatelli in the hallway when he exited the locker room.

"Good morning," she said. "Ready to get started?" *You condescending, white asshole!*

Donatelli zeroed in on Holmes's eyes, which regarded him coolly, almost warily. She'd grown dramatically less attractive, too.

Feeling a flash of anger, Donatelli decided not to broach his conversation with Anders. He would wait and see if Holmes said something first.

Sure, Holmes had saved his life, but that was her job. He'd save a total stranger in a heartbeat, because that's what he was supposed to do. Protect and serve.

"Let's roll," Donatelli said simply. "Meet you downstairs in the garage after El Tee briefs us." *You drama-loving, black bitch!*

Hoping his face didn't reflect his annoyance and pain, Donatelli thought of something he was itching to scribble on Holmes's performance evaluation: "Does not play well with others . . ."

⌒⌒

HARDLY A SLAVE TO FASHION, Darryl Billups stood in front of a clothing store mirror, admiring himself in his new threads. Left with no option after last night's fire, he'd broken down and bought himself two pairs of slacks costing seventy dollars apiece, as well as two long-sleeve shirts that could be worn for business or casually.

Capping off his unprecedented shopping spree, Darryl also purchased two pairs of socks and underwear. And a belt. That should hold him until he could return to his house and access his smoke-filled duds.

Darryl smiled sheepishly at his reflection, realizing it had been at least a year since his last clothing purchase. Like many men, Darryl found shopping for clothes synonymous with Chinese water torture.

The salesgirl assisting Darryl was attractive and flirtatious, taking pains to brush up against Darryl on at least two occasions. But she was wasting her time—although he noticed her and was flattered, his relationship with Yolanda was a wound on his heart at the moment. Not to mention his psyche.

Darryl stepped out of the downtown Baltimore clothing store looking snazzy in his new duds. Darryl smiled, feeling his trademark confidence and optimism beginning to return. Both had taken a major hit the previous night.

No sense getting bent out of shape about the fire, because his belongings were insured. And if anything irreplaceable— like pictures—had been destroyed, that's just the way it was. The important thing was, Darryl was alive and healthy to make new pictures. It was amazing, the degree to which a good night's rest could improve one's outlook.

On a day like this, under different circumstances he might have been sorely tempted to find a butcher shop and buy about ten chicken necks for a nickel apiece. Next he would wrap a length of twine around each neck, then drive down to

South Baltimore, where the Potee Street bridge crosses a tributary of the Patapsco River.

Given today's pretty weather, there were probably already scores of men and women hanging over the side of the bridge, wearing hats to block the sun and dangling chicken necks into the warm, slow-moving water. In no time a blue crab would be greedily nibbling at the bait, and they're such single-minded creatures that it's easy to hoist the chicken neck out of the water with the crab still attached to it.

One time, Darryl and Mad Dawg had taken a leisurely mental health day and spent about four hours crabbing and shooting the breeze at the Potee Street bridge. At one point, they'd spied an approaching *Baltimore Herald* paper truck and fled into nearby Cherry Hill Park, giggling like truant schoolboys.

Sitting at a stoplight, watching downtown pedestrians as they basked in the glorious weather, Darryl promised himself there would be a Potee Street visit in his immediate future. He would even take a day off, if necessary, because it was starting to dawn on Darryl that playing hard was just as important as working hard.

For the time being, however, work was priority number one. It would be nice to have a metaphorical chicken neck that would make the secrets of the Safe&Sound case come to him like so many blue crabs.

Sitting in his car with the windows rolled down, Darryl was surrounded by the sights and sounds of downtown urban life, attractive young women decked out in short skirts, the distant roar of ships gliding into and out of the port of Baltimore.

Darryl thought of Camille, whom he had sworn he wouldn't utter another word to. Thanks to the Safe&Sound case, it was starting to look as though Darryl would have to break his self-imposed moratorium on calling Camille. She had an off-and-on relationship with one of the few black assistant ME's in the medical examiner's office. Darryl needed another pair of eyes and ears in the ME's office, and Dr. Malik Shaw would do just fine, if he would agree to go along with the program.

Sighing, Darryl pulled out his cellular phone. Things like pride and holding a grudge could never be allowed to block a good story. Eager to have the deed over and done with, he quickly dialed the number to Camille's prestigious downtown law firm. The phone only rang once before Camille's no-nonsense secretary pounced on it.

"Camille Billups's office, may I help you?"

Darryl hesitated for a split second, on the verge of hanging up. Having to ask Camille for a favor was some damned unpleasant medicine. As his father was all too fond of saying, "Never say never."

"Hi, Estelle, this is Darryl. Can I speak to Camille please?"

"Darryl, how are you? I'll see if I can locate her."

Darryl wound up waiting for about two minutes, listening to some horrible easy-listening FM station being piped into the law firm's phone system. A Neil Diamond ditty was just getting cranked up when Camille mercifully picked up the phone, sounding remarkably contrite.

"Hey, Darryl," Camille said slowly. "Before you say anything, I just want to apologize for the other day. I just want you to know that I am very sorry and I would never, ever intentionally do anything to hurt you. And I want you to know that I love you."

Just like that, Dinner at the Winslows' was over and forgiven.

"Thanks, Cee Bee," Darryl said, using his pet nickname for Camille, a sign that brother and sister were cool once again. "It's water under the bridge. By the way, me and Yolanda split up anyway. It probably wouldn't have worked."

Camille paused a beat, knowing better than to say anything that might be construed as approving. "Hey, if it's meant to be, it'll work out," she finally said, giving no hint of her strong disapproval of Yolanda.

"Cee Bee, can you help me with something?" Darryl held his breath.

"Anything, big brother. You name it."

"You and Malik Shaw still seeing each other?"

Darryl cringed. It was tacky to break his silence with his sister only because he needed something.

"We take in an art exhibit every now and then, go to the theater . . . nothing serious. You need help with a story?"

Darryl gulped. "Yeah. Yeah, I really do."

"Give me the number where you are and I'll have him call in a few minutes."

"Thanks, Cee Bee. I appreciate it."

Camille laughed. "I'm always here for you, Darryl. I may not always go about it the best way, but I am looking out for you."

Smiling, Darryl hung up. It was good to know Camille wasn't the personification of evil.

Though Darryl had been seated in his car only a few moments, about ten other drivers had driven past during that time, shooting him imploring glances. They craved that most elusive parcel of downtown real estate: An empty parking space. So Darryl slid down in his seat, leaving only the top of his head visible.

The harsh beeping of his cell phone finally signaled an end to his wait. With any luck, Dr. Malik Shaw would be on the line.

"Hello!" Darryl cried out.

"Shaw here," a cautious-sounding voice responded.

"Hey, I'm Camille's brother and—"

"I know and I think I know where this is going," Shaw said, cutting Darryl off. "Don't talk on this line. Meet me at

Camden Yards at twelve-thirty. Over near the center field fence—near the scoreboard with the Coca-Cola sign on it."

"Done deal. See you in a few."

Sticking his transmission into drive, Darryl eased his car from its metered parking spot. It was 11:40 A.M., giving Darryl fifty minutes to poke around before his meeting with Dr. Shaw. *May as well put that time to good use,* he thought. *Let's see if we can find us a Safe&Sound chicken neck.*

Parking about two blocks from the ME's office and three blocks from Camden Yards, Darryl put enough money in the parking meter for two hours, then set off on foot in the general direction of the medical examiner's office once again.

Several of the buildings near the ME's office had security guards posted at the front desk—maybe someone had seen something around the time the body disappeared from the ME's office. Darryl struck out in the first five lobbies he went to.

The sixth was across Pratt Street from the ME's office and had a uniformed, elderly white man with a pronounced smoker's hack and glasses thick enough to see Saturn's moons behind the security desk. The man looked curiously out of place seated behind a high-tech console that had so many dials and television monitors that it looked like mission control for a space shuttle launch.

"Morning, my name is Darryl Billups and I'm a reporter with the *Baltimore Herald.*"

The old-timer cupped a hand to his ear. Darryl repeated himself, fairly shouting the second time.

"You don't have to scream!" the old man snapped, glaring at Darryl, who inadvertently laughed.

"Sorry," he said easily. "Were you working here a couple of nights ago, when that body disappeared from the medical examiner's office?" Darryl had lowered his voice somewhat but was still speaking far louder than usual.

"Lemme see some ID," the elderly security guard wheezed. Darryl produced his press pass and the guard reached for it with a clawlike arthritis-gnarled hand. Then he cleared his throat and spat violently into a trash can under his desk.

Darryl winced.

"You in luck, son," the guard said conspiratorially. "I just did a month of midnights—I don't mind the midnight shift, 'cause Gertrude died six years ago, God bless her soul."

Darryl nodded, looking at his watch. His meeting with Dr. Shaw was coming up in fifteen minutes.

"I don't need daylight and stuff, like you young guys. Fact is, makes my pressure go up and—" The old gent coughed for a brief spell, then stopped. Darryl began to fidget, mindful that the clock was running, as always.

"Anyways, I was working the other night. Outside smokin' a cigarette around three in the morning when a hearse for Washington Funeral Home came out of the ME's. Didn't look like one of their regular drivers, neither."

Darryl could have kissed the silver stubble on the old man's sunken jowls. Instead he settled for a quick "thank you" and set off at a semijog down Pratt Street, toward Orioles Park at Camden Yards. He had five minutes to travel about five blocks.

As he jogged in the brilliant sunshine, out of nowhere came a thought of Yolanda. No question about it—despite their problems and their many differences, Darryl was still in love with her. After sleeping on it, Darryl had decided that Yolanda would never set fire to their former home. Opening up a terrifying question—if she wasn't responsible, who was?

When he was still one hundred yards from the centerfield scoreboard at Camden Yards, Darryl spotted a rotund man wearing a shirt and tie, no sport coat, and an Afro at least two inches long. Dr. Malik Shaw's appearance surprised Darryl because he thought Camille had a thing for tall, athletic types and because, for some reason, Darryl never pictured an assistant medical examiner wearing an Afro.

"So, you're Camille's big brother?" Dr. Shaw said, extending his hand. "Malik Shaw's the name. I've heard an awful lot about you!"

"Most of it isn't true—you know how sisters exaggerate," Darryl said lightly, studying Dr. Shaw's face. Although his demeanor was affable, Darryl sensed an underlying uneasiness.

"I'm not trying to offend you, bro', but can I see some credentials?"

Shrugging, the purported Dr. Shaw slowly pulled out his wallet and fished out a blue-and-gold laminated card that he handed to Darryl. Satisfied he was talking to the genuine article, Darryl apologized.

"The reason I agreed to see you," Dr. Shaw said, jamming his wallet back home, "is to tip you off on something about the body that disappeared. That lady was pregnant—they did a partial autopsy and pulled out a fetus. It looked to be about two months old."

Darryl instantly understood the significance of this—not only could the fetus help ID the dead woman, but it had the father's DNA, too. Thanks to advances in medical technology, a fetus whose conception and death had occurred decades ago now might be able to make a profound statement about the mother's demise.

"Dr. Roth knows?"

"Sure," Dr. Shaw said, waving his hand. "Nothing happens at the ME's he doesn't know about. Just do me a favor and keep my name the hell out of this."

Jackpot! First the security guard's Washington Funeral Home tip, now this! Having abandoned Darryl's personal life, Lady Luck was smiling down on his professional endeavors big-time.

Sensing he could do no wrong today—when it came to

his job, at least—Darryl bid Dr. Shaw farewell. Given the roll Darryl was on, there was one more important lead that he would check out today. But first some pressing personal business awaited.

THE WOMAN WHOSE REMAINS had been found at the Safe&Sound had been cremated and her ashes unceremoniously poured into a plastic lawn-and-leaf bag by undertaker Hubert Washington.

Incredibly, though, a few miles away she was coming back to life. With the same luminous skin, expressive eyes, and immaculately coiffed hair that had always been her trademark.

Her transformation was occurring in a windowless third-floor room at the downtown headquarters of the Baltimore Police Department. Lady S&S may have been incinerated, but she lived on in the hundreds of photographs that homicide investigators had taken of her body.

Robbed of a corpse to work with, homicide lieutenant Tuck Anders decided to do the next best thing—have a police department sketch artist look at photos of the Safe&Sound victim, then do a rendering of how she probably appeared alive.

That drawing would then be circulated among the local media—including Baltimore's television stations, the *Herald*, and the *Afro-American*.

Anders had a hunch that a victim wearing Lady S&S's expensive jewelry would be remembered—and missed—by quite a few people. So a female sketch artist working from four-color photographs of Lady S&S's body busily began re-creating her likeness on a sketch pad.

Once a basic outline had been mapped out, watercolors were added to approximate Lady S&S's skin tone, hair color, and even the shade of lipstick she was wearing when she died. The finished result was uncannily on the mark.

Lady S&S would get her first unveiling on the eleven o'clock news tonight. Looking over the sketch artist's shoulder, Anders smiled, imagining the jolt a few select viewers would receive when they turned on their television sets.

What could possibly be more unnerving than to kill someone, hide her body, then see the dead person's smiling face beaming over the airwaves nearly two decades later?

CHAPTER 13

Funeral director Hubert Washington gazed back and forth between the hard, uncompromising faces of homicide detectives Scott Donatelli and Thelma Holmes. Their unmarked white Chevrolet subcompact was parked in the driveway of the Washington Funeral Home when Washington pulled up, driving one of his cream-colored hearses. It was the same vehicle that had carried Adrienne Jackson's body to his establishment to be cremated. Washington had just returned from having the vehicle detailed where he requested that the interior be cleaned with industrial-strength solvents, then vacuumed twice.

The owner of the car wash had charged Washington seventy-five dollars for an interior and exterior cleaning and wax and had gratefully pocketed a fifty-dollar tip from Washington. There was nothing unusual about the appearance of Washington, a regular customer at the detailing shop, or about his request.

Washington's tip had raised eyebrows, though, because it was the first one he'd left in five years.

The moment Donatelli and Holmes stepped from their vehicle and began walking toward him, Washington knew precisely who they were and why they were at his establishment. He must have taken leave of his senses, thinking he could casually burn a human body as if it were a pile of autumn leaves.

But far from being frightened or concerned, Washington felt self-assured, even cocky. Because if these cops could find any trace of Adrienne Jackson within the small amount of intermingled remains inside his crematory, then these two were damned good. Without a body, they didn't have shit.

"Hubert Washington—can I help you two?" Washington said easily, striding toward Donatelli and Holmes as they approached him. Both of them had a vaguely pissed-off aura about them. There would be no bad cop/good cop routine here, just two prickly pigs.

Too bad, because the black female cop would be kind of cute if she simply smiled a bit, Washington noted.

"We're working a homicide where the victim was stashed in a self-storage facility," Holmes said, never moving her light brown eyes from Washington's face. "The body disappeared from the medical examiner's office."

"Yeah, I saw it in the paper," Washington said with a touch of impatience.

"One of your hearses was seen leaving the basement of the medical examiner's office around the same time the victim's body disappeared," Holmes said, narrowing her eyes.

"Yeah, your hearse was seen by a night watchman *and*

by a video surveillance camera," Donatelli said, embellishing things a bit. "Can you tell us what it was doing there?"

Oh shit, oh shit, oh shit! They know already!

Washington shrugged. "My hearses go all over the Baltimore metropolitan area. Nothing unusual about that."

Blood was in the water and Holmes and Donatelli both sensed it.

"Your hearse was the only one seen leaving the ME's office from midnight until seven A.M.," Donatelli said, lying again. "Got somethin' you wanna tell us?"

Looking down at his shoes, Washington let out a long breath. "Yeah, I do have something to tell both of you."

Donatelli kept twirling his toothpick between his lips, his dark eyes unreadable behind aviator glasses. Meanwhile, Holmes's expression conveyed a mixture of skepticism and boredom.

"What I have to tell you is this: I have work to do and if you aren't going to arrest me, get your car out of my driveway. I need to do my job!"

Holmes smiled, startling Washington with her show of pearly whites. "It would be real embarrassing if your business misplaced somebody's loved one, right?" she said sweetly. "Well, that's kind of what happened to us, and we're looking pretty stupid here."

Holmes's grin grew even wider. "I really do hate to look stupid, Mr. Washington." The detective's smile disappeared.

"Being an accessory to murder is some serious shit," she said sternly. "In a case like this, you probably wouldn't even be eligible for parole until you served twenty, twenty-five years. What would that make you—seventy-five, eighty years old?

"So here's the deal—you can cooperate and tell us what you know, or we can return with a warrant. If that happens, I promise you we'll take your hearses and your building apart screw by screw. Your choice."

Holmes's right earlobe was throbbing as she spoke, putting a little extra gusto into her words.

Washington hesitated, weighing whether or not to spill the beans and save his own hide. The possibility that there might be a videotape showing his hearse leaving the medical examiner's office was extremely troubling. That would be hard to explain.

Badly shaken now, Washington decided to hold firm. The detectives would still have to prove their case, which wouldn't be easy. Anyway, a friend in high places had gotten him into this mess—maybe that same friend could get him out.

"Come back with a warrant," Washington said in a loud show of false bravado. "Until then, both of you can kiss my black ass!" With that, he marched up the sunshine-drenched concrete driveway of his funeral home and went inside.

Donatelli and Holmes stood in the driveway and watched Washington depart before returning to their car. Both sat and stared hard and long at the converted house Washington worked out of, as if halfway expecting him to come dashing back outside with a tearful confession on his lips.

Holmes literally bit her lower lip. Why had Donatelli lied about the video camera? Hunkering down in her seat, Holmes crossed her arms and looked out the passenger window.

She had promised herself she would work with the homicide squad at least one year. But there was no way she could endure an entire year of Scott Donatelli.

Meanwhile, in his office inside the Washington Funeral Home, Hubert Washington was also thinking about career decisions. Once and for all, he would put an end to the drama surrounding the secret cremation he'd performed.

Reaching into the top drawer of his desk, Washington pulled out his American Express gold card. Then he turned on his computer and logged into an on-line discount travel site. Washington booked a round-trip flight to the Dominican

Republic that left from Baltimore-Washington International Airport the following morning and was slated to return a week later.

Over the years, he'd quietly funneled $300,000 into Dominican offshore bank accounts. Enough to live like Latin royalty if he chose not to return to the States.

Given that his kids were grown and that he didn't even particularly like—much less love—his wife and was weary of the funeral business, Washington had little incentive to return from his spur-of-the-moment overseas excursion.

He had no clue how to apply for a Dominican visa, but he'd worry about that later.

WHEN FLAMES RAMPAGE through a house they burn much more than furniture, clothing, and roofing tiles. A chunk of someone's life always gets cauterized in the process, too. Not only do house fires show life at its most capricious, but they also demonstrate humankind's helplessness against the most basic of elements, Darryl Billups thought as he surveyed the blackened ruins of his living room.

Music CDs that he'd amassed since 1985 were now welded together, a gray river of plastic had stopped in midflow as it ran down a metal CD tower. The Molotov cocktail hurled through his living room window had scored a direct hit on Darryl's photo albums under the coffee table. Photographic memories chronicling Darryl's life from infancy to adulthood were now ashes, under the skeleton of a coffee table.

Everything in the living room—from Darryl's stereo to his art deco Lava lamp—was either blackened, charred, or melted from the tremendous heat and smoke of the fire. And whatever hadn't been affected by heat and smoke had been damaged by water.

A pungent, eye-watering aroma of burning plastic permeated every corner of the house. And in the living room was the faint, unmistakable odor of gasoline.

Darryl's neck tingled under the collar of his new shirt, but there was no sense in getting angry. It wouldn't restore his damaged belongings or otherwise help get his life back to normal. Still, he couldn't help himself—the longer he stayed inside his home, the more pissed he became.

So he did a slow burn while dealing with the fire department arson investigator and an adjuster from his insurance company. Both were straightforward and didn't direct any pity or sympathy toward Darryl, for which he was grateful.

Then they left to deal with someone else's life-altering event, leaving Darryl to grope with his. He didn't want to spend another second inside the home where he'd broken up with his fianceé, then become the victim of a firebomb. Moving about rapidly, gathering several loads of smoke-cured clothing, an alarm clock, and a few books, Darryl hurriedly made his way to the car.

Then he drove off without looking back.

It would take a minimum of four weeks before the house would be ready for Darryl to move back in, the insurance woman guessed.

He had honored his promise to himself and hadn't mentioned Yolanda's name while talking to the arson investigator. Well, that wasn't totally true—he had mentioned that they had just broken up, but he didn't single Yolanda out as a potential suspect.

As bad as Darryl felt, he couldn't get too bent out of shape over losing material things in the fire. Bottom line, he wasn't lying in a hospital bed needing skin grafts, relying on a ventilator to inflate fire-damaged lungs.

He was still pissed, though.

THE SAME FEMALE Maryland state trooper who had been on duty yesterday was still in the lobby when Darryl came barging through the glass doors. She gave him another piercing once-over.

"Yessir, can I help you?"

"I want to see Dr. Roth again please," Darryl said confidently, prompting the state trooper to blink in amazement. "Tell him his job is on the line, because I *know* about the fetus!"

The trooper started to respond, but Darryl merely held up his hand. "Time is wasting—I don't think he'd appreciate getting fired just because I was denied access."

Once again by himself in the medical examiner's building, Darryl looked around the lobby. The wall near the elevators was made of black granite and etched into it, in gold block letters, was a phrase from Hippocrates: "Wherever the Art of Medicine is practiced there is also a love of humanity."

Darryl found that odd in a building devoted to the dead. Opposite the elevators was a group of three-by-five, black-and-white photographs of chief medical examiners past and present. In the foyer near the front doors was a small picture of Maryland's governor.

"I didn't vote for him—did you?"

Darryl turned to find himself face-to-face with Dr. Roth, who looked none too pleased to have a nosy member of the press poking around inside his building again.

"Let's talk in my office," Dr. Roth said, grabbing hold of Darryl's elbow and guiding him down the hall. Homicide detectives Thelma Holmes and Scott Donatelli were already seated on the sofa in Dr. Roth's office when Darryl arrived.

Closing the door, Dr. Roth motioned for Darryl to have a seat also, but Darryl ignored him and remained standing. He glanced briefly at the cops before launching into Dr. Roth. "Why didn't you tell me you guys cut a fetus out of the Safe&Sound corpse?" Darryl asked angrily.

Dr. Roth cringed at the mention of the word *fetus*. Holmes's and Donatelli's jaws dropped. "Who told you that?" Dr. Roth asked, smoothing his hair.

Darryl noticed the doctor was shaking. "That's not important," Darryl shot back. "*You* should have told me."

Dr. Roth appeared at a loss for words. He sat behind his desk and aimlessly rearranged some paperwork. Then he cleared his throat a couple of times as everyone in the office looked at him, waiting for an end to the unbearable silence in the room.

"You need to keep this development out of your story, Darryl." It was Donatelli who finally spoke. "Please don't write about the fetus."

Darryl looked at Donatelli as if he had lost his mind. "Last time I looked, the *Baltimore Herald* was signing my paychecks, Scott. Why the hell shouldn't I report that this woman was pregnant?"

"Because you will blow our investigation to hell, that's why," Donatelli replied gravely, removing the trademark toothpick and stroking his goatee. "Simple as that."

Roth, Holmes, and Donatelli all gazed at Darryl. Darryl knew he held the upper hand and had no intention of squandering his advantage without getting something in return. Something significant.

"You've gotta do a helluva lot better than that, Scott," Darryl laughed. "What's in it for me?"

Donatelli's eyes rolled and he slowly tilted his head toward the ceiling. This Safe&Sound case was already screwed up enough without a reporter being privy to sensitive information, the detective thought. Not only couldn't the ME's office keep track of bodies; now it was leaking critical information also.

Donatelli rose abruptly from Dr. Roth's couch and strode across the chief medical examiner's office, his mane of black hair flowing behind him. "Can you come outside for a sec, Darryl?" Donatelli made no effort to hide his disgust, nor did Darryl try to disguise his delight as he followed the detective out the door and into the hallway.

With his back to Darryl, Donatelli gazed briefly at the framed black-and-white photos of past medical examiners that hung on the wall near Dr. Roth's office. Then he turned dramatically, moved closer to Darryl, and began speaking in a hushed voice.

"You turning into a clotheshorse on me, my man?" Donatelli said, eyeing Darryl's hip new clothes. The young homicide detective definitely had an eye for detail—he didn't miss a trick.

Darryl smiled slightly, waiting for Donatelli to cut to the chase. The two of them had interacted on a high-profile murder case before, and Darryl liked the young detective, respected his ability. However, if Donatelli had nothing to offer in return for holding the fetus development, Darryl wasn't going to wait for Baltimore's other newspapers and television stations to stumble upon it.

"Whatcha got for me, Scott? Tee it up."

"Nothing right now, Darryl, but give me twenty-four hours and I swear I'll tighten you up with some good stuff. I swear." Standing in the hallway, which was lit by ghoulish fluorescent lighting, Darryl noticed that Donatelli was gritting his teeth as if in pain.

Cooperating with Donatelli now might pay dividends down the road, Darryl reasoned. But empty promises don't cut it in police work or in journalism. You gotta deliver the goods or get off the pot. Not only was the fetus story too juicy to sit on, but Darryl was eager to stick it to Dr. Roth.

"Sorry, Scott, but I'm gonna have to run with this one. It's too good to pass up."

Donatelli shrugged and sucked on his toothpick, but his

face remained impassive. "Okay, have it your way," he said simply. Then he eased open the door to Dr. Roth's office and slid back inside.

Roth's and Holmes's eyes were boring into Darryl when he reentered the room. Donatelli, seated on the couch with Holmes, folded his hands in his lap and merely stared at the opposite wall. Darryl felt like hopping up on Dr. Roth's desk and beating his chest in triumph.

Instead, he walked up to an overstuffed leather chair in front of Dr. Roth's desk and plopped down in it as if he owned it. Darryl took out his microcassette recorder, turned it on, and placed it beside a beautiful crystal paperweight on Dr. Roth's desk.

"Tell me about the fetus please, Dr. Roth," Darryl said.

Dr. Roth looked imploringly at Donatelli, who shrugged his shoulders, then leaned back on the sofa to take in the show.

"It appears to have been about two months old when its mother died," Dr. Roth said slowly, looking pale. "We've conducted a preliminary toxicology test and there's no evidence of drugs in its body."

"Is it valuable from a DNA standpoint?"

"Potentially . . . yes. Very much so." Dr. Roth sent another silent SOS to Donatelli, who crossed his legs and mouthed the word "stop" twice.

"Did the police get skin samples from beneath the victim's nails?"

Donatelli had finally had enough. "Time to bring this bullshit to an end," he barked. "Darryl, you need to be moving on. If you think we're going to sit here and go over the details of my investigation, you've lost your fucking mind."

"Don't cuss at me," Darryl said in a low voice. "And butt out, because I wasn't talking to you anyway."

Donatelli rose slowly from the couch. "Tell you what— this is a crime scene. It's about time for you to leave."

"Yeah," Dr. Roth chimed in, remaining seated. "I was just getting ready to say that."

Darryl casually removed his tape recorder from Dr. Roth's desk, then turned and looked at Holmes, Donatelli, and Dr. Roth, holding each person's gaze.

"So, that's how it's gonna be?"

"Afraid so," Holmes said.

"And this is supposed to stop me from reporting this story?" Darryl snorted. "Dream on."

Darryl walked out of Roth's office and out of the building. Outside, he encountered a magnificent salmon-colored sky dotted with wispy pink clouds, the result of the sun and the approaching dusk beginning their daily tug-of-war. Dr. Malik Shaw happened to be coming out at the same time, his Afro turned reddish by the sinking sun.

"You don't know me!" Dr. Shaw hissed under his breath as he walked toward a filthy late-model, blue Mercedes sedan.

"Call me on my cell phone," Darryl murmured, certain Dr. Roth was watching from his office window.

Darryl was about to open the door to his car when he noticed movement out of the corner of his eye.

He froze and, sure enough, the sound of air rushing from a tire could be heard coming from the other side of his car. Darryl hurtled to the other side of his car, and an enormous figure wearing a dark shirt and light-colored slacks rose and began to sprint toward Pratt Street at a breakneck pace.

Darryl was in good shape and a pretty fast runner, but the athletic man he was trailing quickly pulled out a ten-yard advantage, then turned down Pratt Street, in the direction of the Inner Harbor.

"Hey, stop, you son of a bitch! Stop!" Darryl hollered, feeling a burning sensation creep into his calves and thighs.

He covered a block in no time, legs and arms pumping furiously, his breathing measured and under control.

"Stop, shithead!" Whoever Darryl was chasing was one fast bastard because, in the span of one block, he had pulled out another twenty feet on Darryl and was continuing to ease away.

Although, on one level, Darryl knew he was engaged in the act of running and could see his quarry directly in front of him, this afternoon pursuit down Pratt Street had an air of unreality to it. This had to be a dream, a nightmare he couldn't wake from. But the burning in his legs was telling him otherwise.

The tire vandal ducked into a shadow-filled alley to his left and Darryl followed suit at top speed. He had taken four, maybe five steps when he saw a couple of orange muzzle flashes ahead and heard a booming report that sounded like an artillery piece inside the narrow alley.

Throwing his hands in front of his face, as if that would somehow deflect a bullet streaking toward him, Darryl skidded to a stop and began zigzagging madly out of the alley and back in the direction of the medical examiner's building.

A lawman in a campus police vehicle happened to be driving past the alley Darryl raced out of as two shots rang out. The cop abruptly slammed on his brakes and backed his vehicle onto the sidewalk, near the grimy alley entranceway. After getting on his radio and requesting backup, the officer bounded from his car and unholstered his side arm.

The alley and Pratt Street were soon swarming with campus and city police cars, but they had no luck locating Darryl's assailant. They did find his calling card, though—two brass-colored 9mm shells that had tinkled to the ground near a trash can.

The shots were fired so quickly that Darryl didn't have

time to get scared. He'd often wondered what ran through the minds of homicide victims being used for target practice by some miscreant. Now Darryl knew the answer: Not a dog-gone thing, except survival.

There had been no epiphanies, no sudden answers to the question of the meaning of life. Nothing had crossed through Darryl's mind. After he saw the muzzle flashes, the instinc-tual part of his brain had taken over, totally overriding the cerebral segment used for thinking.

Suddenly, a powerful hand clutched Darryl's shoulder through the open window of the squad car, and he nearly jumped out of his skin trying to move away from it.

The hand belonged to homicide detective Thelma Holmes, who had jogged up the street along with Scott Donatelli to see what the commotion was all about.

"You okay?" she asked in a husky voice.

Darryl looked at Holmes and confirmed the impressions he had formed at the door of her home—Holmes was a very attractive woman. "Yeah, I'm fine. The hit man you guys hired didn't have very good aim."

Holmes smiled. A little one, but it was genuine. "See you around, Darryl," she said gruffly, turning to walk away.

"Wait a minute."

Holmes turned on her heel, eyebrows arched. Looking at her big-boned frame, for some reason Darryl wondered what Holmes would look like after a baby or two.

"Can't you see I'm in danger here?" Darryl asked in mock terror. "I need police protection—help a brother out!"

This time, Holmes gave a little laugh that made her full bosom quiver. Little flirtatious exchanges can be annoying as hell or quite intriguing, depending on who's doing the flirt-ing. Most men were thoroughly intimidated by her line of work, so it was nice to be flirted with for a change.

"No way," she said simply. "Scott and I are a little busy here, in case you hadn't noticed."

Donatelli stood beside Holmes, saying nothing and frowning slightly, like a disapproving lover. Darryl couldn't have cared less. He noticed that Holmes hadn't walked away yet and that was all he was concerned with.

Maybe he was in shock from being shot at or trying to rebound from Yolanda or just reacting to the incredible stress of the last couple of days. But for some reason, Darryl suddenly found himself quite interested in Thelma Holmes.

And what better place to meet a cute female cop than surrounded by blinking squad cars while giving information for a police report?

"Come on; we're not finished at the medical examiner's office," Donatelli said brusquely to Holmes. Then, glancing at Darryl, Donatelli muttered, "Glad you're okay."

A sudden burst of rebelliousness surged through Holmes. Did it really make any difference if she spent a couple of seconds checking on Darryl? Not really—Donatelli was all about being in control, being in charge. And the last man to successfully control Thelma Holmes was her father, God rest his soul.

"We can talk some night after work, but not tonight."

"Tomorrow night, then. At the Kit-Kat Club, ten o'clock."

Holmes grinned, appreciating two things about her exchange with Darryl. Number one: It appeared to be irritating the hell out of Donatelli, who patted his foot impatiently and practically gnawed his toothpick in half as he waited. Number two: She liked aggressive men who had a pretty clear idea of what they wanted and where they were going. All of those criterion appeared to apply to Darryl. So far, anyway.

"Deal," she said.

Still seated in the University of Maryland police car, Darryl turned triumphantly toward the cop taking his police report.

"Watch out for female police officers, bro'," giving a high five to Darryl. "I guess you know most of them are lesbos, right?"

Darryl didn't bother to respond. Instead, he let his thoughts drift to his impending encounter with Holmes. Given that he was now being shot at and his property vandalized on a regular basis, Darryl hoped that he would still be around to meet her the following night.

After detailing the circumstances surrounding the attempted shooting, Darryl arranged to have the *Baltimore Herald* vehicle whose tires had been flattened, towed.

Then he caught a cab to the newspaper and was halfway finished writing his story when the computer system crashed, on deadline no less. The first edition of the paper was thirty minutes late, causing frayed nerves in the newsroom.

Once his writing duties had been successfully discharged, Darryl set out to scratch an itch that had been tormenting him all day. He walked to the newspaper's library, a repository of old clippings, microfilm, and reference materials for editors and reporters.

Darryl asked the night librarian to give him the files for every missing person story published by the *Herald* from 1980 through 1989. Her search yielded 147 stories, most of them mercifully a few paragraphs in length. Those focusing on missing males could be ignored, making Darryl's task somewhat easier. He managed to race through the stories for the years 1980, '81, '82, and '83 in about thirty minutes.

Darryl was midway through 1984 when a phrase from a yellowed newspaper clipping in his hand leapt out: "Was last seen wearing a bracelet with an eighteen-karat white gold mounting and fifty-six princess-cut diamonds, along with a two-karat gold, platinum, and diamond engagement ring."

Darryl sat up in his chair and blinked. The story was about the disappearance of Adrienne Jackson, a well-known chanteuse in small nightclubs in Baltimore and Washington. She had a touch for singing jazz songs that made audiences wonder why she hadn't signed a major record deal yet.

Prior to her music career, Jackson had yearned to be a model but was repeatedly rebuffed. Not because she lacked beauty. However, at five-foot-five she was considered too short in stature for runway work.

The piece ran on April 23, 1984, and was accompanied by a picture of a beautiful, dark-skinned woman with perfect white teeth, a heart-shaped face and shoulder-length, dark hair. But a sentence in the story's last paragraph literally caused Darryl to leap to his feet.

"Ms. Jackson is the fiancée of prominent city business lawyer and city councilman Charles Hudson." Darryl started dancing the cabbage patch inside the *Herald*'s library, which definitely caught the night librarian by surprise. Could it be that the stiff found in the Safe&Sound was Charles Hudson's fiancée?

"Oh, my God!" Darryl sprinted out to the newsroom to tell a night editor what he'd discovered. They agreed there wasn't enough substantiation to warrant placing Darryl's scoop into late editions of the newspaper. "But I'll take a shot at nailing it down tomorrow, for sure," Darryl promised.

AFTER DUSK, the skies of Baltimore are lit by so many street lamps and headlights that it's difficult to view the artistry Mother Nature bestows on a starry, moonlit night. Therefore, it was a rare treat for Darryl to lean back and take in the Milky Way and the constellations, as seen from Druid Hill Park.

His fellow stargazer was none other than Mad Dawg Murdoch, who had driven to the city park in his red Italian convertible with its distinctive WHAZZUP license tags.

Darryl had insisted that they go to Druid Hill to get away from the city's regular hustle and bustle. Not to mention a potential encounter with whoever had cut the tires on the *Baltimore Herald* vehicle earlier in the day, then sent two 9mm bullets winging his way.

Leery of driving his own car or a *Baltimore Herald* vehicle, Darryl had asked Mad Dawg to handle the driving duties. More than anything, Darryl needed to laugh, to talk to someone skilled at pointing out life's absurdities. Whenever that was the case, Mad Dawg usually had just the prescription.

Darryl started to mention what he'd appeared to have uncovered about the Safe&Sound murder, but opted not to. This wasn't a night for shoptalk—tonight was about finding a safe haven in the companionship of a close friend.

Gazing into the untold depths of the night sky had a calming effect on Darryl. He and his problems were but a microscopic fleck of dust in the grand scheme of things. "And don't you forget that, either!" Darryl said quietly.

Mad Dawg slowly turned from a cluster of stars near the western horizon and took a long, hard look at his homeboy.

"You ain't flippin' out on me, is you?" Dawg asked with a mischievous grin. "Don't start speaking to yourself and talking in tongues and shit. You my boy and all that, but I'll commit yo' ass in a heartbeat!"

"Dawg."

"Yeah, boy!"

"Shut the hell up."

They laughed and continued to pour a bottle of cheap wine into two plastic cups.

Totally comfortable with each other and their friendship, Darryl and Mad Dawg said nothing for several minutes and just admired the stars. Within an hour, Mad Dawg had sworn up and down he'd seen at least five planets.

Darryl scoffed at each purported sighting, and they roared with laugher after Mad Dawg claimed to see a space shuttle sailing through the far reaches of space.

The viselike tension and pressure Darryl had been under gradually dropped away like the layers of an onion. And as Darryl began to feel more and more relaxed, he gradually unburdened. He revealed his breakup with Yolanda and the arson at his home.

Dawg had been vaguely insulted to learn Darryl hadn't leaned on him for support earlier. But that was Darryl's way—despite what he did for a living, he was basically a private person. He had a tendency to let things out and allow people in slowly and on his own terms.

Yolanda repeatedly told Darryl that he had a way of analyzing things to death, instead of just going with the flow. Maybe on that count, at least, she was right.

"Lemme know if I'm getting too personal here, kid," Mad Dawg said. "But why do you think Yolanda kicked you to the curb like that, boy?"

Darryl took another swig of wine. The muscles in his back and neck felt like braided wires—a massage sure would be right on time. Yolanda had a way of massaging him from head to toe that nearly left him limp when she finished. It didn't thrill Darryl to think that Boone might possibly be getting one of those magic massages at that very moment.

Then Darryl recalled the massages he used to give Yolanda. Usually administered with body oils, candles, a Will Downing CD, and a chilled bottle of Asti Spumante. The rubdowns probably didn't have a lot of therapeutic value, but they were applied so tenderly and sensually that Yolanda used to—

"Yo! Anybody home? You with me, kid?"

Darryl was glad Mad Dawg had jolted him out of his reverie. He didn't need to be remembering that kind of stuff now. It served no purpose except to make him miserable.

"First of all, nobody got kicked to the curb," Darryl said defensively. "Like I said, things broke down on both sides. Each of us needed to make a move."

Mad Dawg took another sip of wine, then fiddled with his car stereo, turning down the volume a bit. Darryl could tell Mad Dawg's curiosity wasn't satisfied.

"Lemme see if I got this straight," Dawg said quietly. "You come home, your lady is gone, and some of your shit is gone, too . . . but you didn't get kicked to the curb?" Dawg erupted into one of his Eddie Murphy belly laughs, and Darryl joined right in. It was irrelevant to him how his breakup with Yolanda was described. It didn't matter who got kicked to the curb, dumped—all the usual relationship buzzwords meant nothing. The important thing was, he was free of an increasingly uncomfortable pairing with a woman he probably would have had a very limited future with.

"Whatever, Dawg. Whatever. I'm a free man, that's all I know. I got saved from making a big mistake."

"But you still love her."

"Do I? What, you got ESP now, bitch?"

Mad Dawg laughed again, this time right in Darryl's face. "Puhleeeze! This Dawg you talkin' to, okay?"

Having enjoyed Mad Dawg's company tremendously up to that point, Darryl found that Dawg was beginning to grate on his nerves.

"Brother, thanks for giving me a shoulder to cry on. Time for me to turn in now," Darryl said with a huge yawn.

Mad Dawg drank the last few ounces of wine directly from the bottle. "You sure you don't want to crash in my spot? Mi casa es su casa, amigo. Plus, we could always hit some more of that chiba chiba, you know."

Clenching his hands, Darryl stretched and unleashed another monstrous yawn. He was in danger of falling asleep if Mad Dawg didn't hurry and drive off.

"You know damn well I wouldn't get any rest because you've always got some freak up in your spot. As for that chiba chiba stuff, I told you I ain't doing that no more. You caught me in a moment of weakness the other night—I'm through."

Mad Dawg nodded. "Have it your way, kid. 'Cause you right, I'm gonna get my freak on tonight. And ain't you or nobody else stoppin' me."

"Take me to my car, fool, and stop wasting time! I can barely stay awake as it is."

Mad Dawg drove Darryl back to the *Baltimore Herald*, where he had arranged to pick up an unmarked company car.

After saying good-bye to Mad Dawg, Darryl drove to Randallstown, a western suburb of Baltimore, where he rented another motel room and fell asleep still wearing his new clothes.

CHAPTER 14

When an eerily lifelike drawing of Adrienne Jackson's lovely face drifted across television sets all over Baltimore, Gregory Hudson wasn't watching the evening news. Like many black men in the city, Hudson could recite chapter and verse what the Ravens or Orioles happened to be up to. But keeping abreast of events and people that actually impacted his life was just a little too painful. Reality can be that way for a black man in America sometimes, making sports, drugs, and alcohol great anesthetics.

So Hudson was semidrunk in an East Baltimore pool hall when Adrienne materialized on thousands of TV screens, along with an impassioned plea from officials to contact police with tips about her identity.

Though Gregory may have been oblivious to the eleven o'clock news, his brother, Charles, couldn't afford to be. Monitoring the news was part of his job, as was occasional spin control. Before Adrienne's picture had faded from Charles Hudson's television screen, he was punching in the numbers to his brother's cell phone.

"Greg, Adrienne's picture was just on television. Her picture was just on the tube," Charles Hudson said quietly. "Everybody in this city over the age of forty will probably remember . . . that she was my fiancée."

"Hold on," Gregory said abruptly. "Eight ball in the *side* pocket, muthafucka!"

Charles Hudson heard momentary silence on the other end of the line, then the sound of clicking pool balls, followed a second later by uproarious laughter and booming male and female voices congratulating Gregory on a successful shot. While Charles's world was disintegrating, little brother was playing a carefree game of billiards!

"Greg! Did you hear what I said, man?"

"Hold on a sec—sumbitch, gimme my goddamn money!"

There was no response for another thirty seconds as a disbelieving Charles Hudson waited for his brother to return to the phone. Once Gregory's collection activities had apparently been satisfied, he got back on the line, sounding remote and unconcerned.

"Whatchoo wan' me to do, man? You just figured out this some serious shit?" Gregory said in a near whisper. His brother had never shed a tear over Adrienne, Gregory recalled. So Gregory would be damned if he would get bent out of shape now.

"Whatchoo wan' me to do?" Gregory said, trying to sound as if he actually cared.

"What do I want you to do?" Charles Hudson screamed. Gregory guessed he was in the den of his ugly brown-and-white Tudor home, with the door closed so his wife wouldn't hear.

"What do I want you to do?" Charles repeated. "What the

fuck could you possibly do now? You've done enough, don't you think?"

Pursing his lips, Gregory Hudson angrily snapped his dainty-looking yellow cell phone shut and dropped it in his pocket.

It was ringing again in about three seconds.

"As long as you're still *black*, don't you ever hang up on me!" Charles Hudson sputtered.

"Whatchoo want?" Gregory grunted. "She was on television—ain't nothin' I can do about it now. You mister answer man, you so goddamn smart. What's the next move, big man?"

This time it was Charles Hudson who hung up. Sinking to his knees in the mahogany-paneled den of his home, he tried unsuccessfully to calm himself before launching into a heart-felt prayer. "Mama, I know you're watching me and I know you love me—and Greg," Charles Hudson said. "And, Mama, I know Greg is my flesh and blood . . . so please forgive me. I beg you, Mama, please forgive me."

Hearing footsteps approaching the locked den door, Hudson quickly popped to his feet.

"Charlie, what are you doing in there? Why did you jump out of bed? Please open the door, sweetie—I'm so, so sorry about Adrienne."

ACROSS THE CITY of Baltimore, phone lines in black households were on fire within minutes after the appearance of Adrienne Jackson's picture.

"Girl, you will never believe who they found after all these years! Adrienne Jackson!"

She had been a beloved figure for most of Baltimore, not just its black community. Club owners in the city, as well as in Annapolis and Washington, had understood that Adrienne and her jazz singing represented a surefire ticket for packing in customers.

As fate would have it, Adrienne had started to become much more than "Baltimore's own" just before she died. She had been developing a strong following in Richmond and Philadelphia. New York couldn't be far behind, and soon Baltimoreans would have another female superstar to claim in addition to Billie Holiday.

But right on the verge of her inevitable ascent to superstardom, Adrienne Jackson unaccountably disappeared. Far from being viewed as a suspect, her boyfriend—lawyer and city councilman Charles Hudson—had been the recipient of a massive outpouring of public sympathy. Total strangers approached him on the street or in city hall to silently hug him or clasp his hand.

Conventional wisdom held that there was no way Charles Hudson could have been involved in her disappearance. Like Adrienne, he was viewed as wholesome, talented, and an integral part of black Baltimore's crème de la crème. When weeks, then months elapsed without any word of Adrienne's whereabouts, her adoring fans slowly came to grips with the likelihood that she was no longer living. A realization made doubly painful by the fact that they had no body or funeral to help hasten closure.

Adrienne and her legacy represented a long-standing, unaddressed ache in the city's psyche. A police sketch of her meant nothing to Baltimore's homicide detectives, most of whom weren't on the force when Adrienne Jackson disappeared in 1984. But her picture triggered a firestorm of recognition among Baltimore television watchers. Phone lines at the city's four major stations were tied up until well after midnight with calls from people correctly identifying the mystery lady found at the Safe&Sound. In their excitement, they'd forgotten to call the police hot-line number all four television stations had flashed under Adrienne Jackson's picture.

The portrait promised to send an electric buzz of gossip and discussion racing through Baltimore, Annapolis, and Washington. The can't-miss jazz superstar, whose mysterious disappearance had broken thousands of hearts, had finally turned up, and she had been murdered. Adding an even more bizarre twist to her story, Adrienne Jackson's body had been stolen from state officials charged with conducting her autopsy.

In addition to being the prime topic of watercooler discussion, Adrienne Jackson's case promised to put a laserlike spotlight on Charles Hudson. People would be curious to see how he would handle the news that his lover had been murdered, and there would probably be another tremendous outpouring of sympathy. Not to mention suspicion, because the disappearance of Adrienne Jackson's body from a government building was a little too convenient.

Darryl Billups had rented his motel room too late to see the evening news. Therefore, he wasn't aware that an artist's rendering had placed Adrienne Jackson's disappearance and death within the orbit of the Honorable Charles Hudson. Just as Darryl had suspected.

PART

DUNGEONS AND DRAGONS

The most outrageous lies that can be invented will
find believers if a man only tells them with all his
might.

—MARK TWAIN

CHAPTER 15

Darting behind a gasoline pump to avoid being seen, Darryl Billups stared at a beautiful, young black woman seated in the front seat of a white Lexus that was getting gas about twenty feet from where he stood.

It was Yolanda, and she was with Boone.

Was Yolanda on the rebound? Darryl wondered, not paying attention to his own car and overfilling the tank, gassing the side of his car. Was she with Boone simply because he was Jamal's father? Or maybe she'd always had a thing for Boone and Darryl had just been something to do until the real thing returned.

Never having experienced low self-esteem during the time he was with Yolanda, Darryl now seemed to be a quivering mass of insecurities.

"Don't do this to yourself, man—she ain't worth the self-doubt," Darryl muttered to himself, looking sheepishly at the gasoline he'd spilled on the ground. Replacing the nozzle, Darryl peeked around the pump one more time. This time he could see Jamal snoozing in the backseat of Boone's car, with no seat belt on.

That was exactly the kind of dumb-ass move Darryl expected from Boone, who stood preening in the humid morning air wearing a white wife-beater as he filled his gas tank. The better to let the world see the massive biceps the thick-headed moron had built from weight lifting.

Jamal was a bright, somewhat precocious kid, who would never receive much in the way of intellectual stimulation from Boone, Darryl thought sadly. He would probably raise Jamal to be a self-absorbed, violence-prone black male, incapable of respecting women or anyone else. Just like Boone.

Out from behind the gas pump a second longer than he'd intended, Darryl was alarmed to see that Yolanda had spotted him and was staring directly into his eyes. For what seemed like an eternity Darryl stood at the gas pump, his hand frozen on the nozzle as he and Yolanda gazed at each other.

For all her faults, Yolanda was still an exquisite woman, with arching cheekbones that were a sculptor's dream, incredibly expressive almond-shaped eyes, short wavy brown hair, and full, luscious lips accentuated by gold lipstick. She had a pensive, almost sad look on her face, instead of the arrogant smirk Darryl half expected. Certain that she had Darryl's attention, she did something he would never forget—after peering toward the back of the Lexus to make sure Boone wasn't looking, Yolanda looked back toward Darryl and mouthed the words "I love you."

Not quite sure how to deal with that, Darryl gave Yolanda a wan smile. He mouthed "good luck" in return and took a final peek in the backseat where an unrestrained Jamal was sleeping peacefully, then turned and walked in the opposite direction. Probably never to see Yolanda or Jamal again.

The hair on Darryl's neck tingled as he remembered how Yolanda and Jamal had fled to Darryl's place after enduring physical abuse from Boone.

God, whatever else happens, please don't let Boone hurt Yolanda or Jamal. Please!

Lunchtime came and went before Darryl could purge Yolanda's words, or the image of her face, from his mind.

He thought about her the entire time he was at the Washington Funeral Home, where no one had answered the front door for the second day in a row. During a meeting with three of his editors at the *Herald*, Darryl looked around the table and saw Yolanda sitting there in triplicate, a damned daunting sight!

It got so bad that Darryl had to snap off his car radio, because every song that came on reminded him of Yolanda. Even jingles for damn commercials. Was he still in love with her after the way she had acted?

If only she hadn't mouthed "I love you." It would be so much easier to hate her if she hadn't done that.

But in a way, the episode at the gas station was helpful. Because the instant Yolanda mouthed those wonderful words, Darryl understood that whatever she was trying to accomplish with Boone was all about Jamal. And nothing else.

Darryl drew an enormous amount of solace from that realization. He felt whole. Mad Dawg was right: Darryl's self-esteem had taken a hit from coming home and discovering his woman and her beloved son had abandoned him.

He would never admit that to Mad Dawg or anyone else, though. A man who shared his weaknesses and vulnerabilities too freely was practically begging for someone to come along and cripple him.

Darryl gathered his silver microcassette recorder, two

ballpoint pens, and trusty notepad from his top desk drawer and set out for the mayor's office, four blocks away.

Mayor Hudson had apparently decided to tackle the Adrienne Jackson controversy head-on, as he had, to Darryl's surprise, agreed to meet with him for a one-on-one interview.

Already wearing a light blue shirt and a yellow tie, all Darryl needed was a sport jacket. He strolled toward the sports department to see if Mad Dawg had a jacket he could borrow.

So many free spirits gravitated toward the sports department, where kegs of beer sometimes magically appeared around midnight. Other *Herald* reporters referred to the section as the Zoo.

One of its denizens was sitting at his desk with earphones on, gold-and-brown dreadlocks bobbing furiously as he penned yet another graceful sports column. Along with everything else that John "Mad Dawg" Murdoch was, he was a tremendously gifted writer constantly looking for ways to perfect his craft.

"Whazzup, boy?" Mad Dawg called out, yanking off his headphones and pushing away from the keyboard. "What's shaking?"

"Man, I gotta go see Hudson and I don't have a jacket—got one?"

Standing up, Mad Dawg looked Darryl up and down twice, then smiled. "You ain't got enough flava to wear my stuff, Bob Dole. Your square ass couldn't handle the vibe flowin' outta my jacket. Son, you just don't—"

"Spare me the shit, Dawg, okay? Gotta meet the mayor in fifteen minutes—do you have a jacket or don't you?"

Still grinning, Mad Dawg walked theatrically toward the sports department's coat closet. "Let's see what awaits behind door number three!" he said, pulling the door open grandly.

Surveying the closet's contents with comical disdain, Mad Dawg smiled suddenly and pulled a lightweight double-breasted gray sport jacket from a hanger. Then he proceeded to dust it off with exaggerated care, picking pieces of lint from the garment here and there.

Darryl impatiently snatched the jacket from Mad Dawg's long, bony fingers, then made his way toward the elevator at a full sprint.

"Thank you, fool!" Darryl shouted over his shoulder.

"There's a nominal rental fee!" Dawg's voice came echoing down the hallway just as the doors to the elevator eased shut.

Darryl flew through the *Herald*'s lobby and out the front door, hitting the streets a little after 1:00 P.M. The air was hot and humid, precisely what one would expect of an August afternoon in Baltimore. At least it was overcast, meaning there was no broiling sun to contend with. The last couple of days had taught Darryl to be thankful for any blessings, regardless of how small.

As soon as he turned down the one-way street the *Herald* was located on, it dawned on Darryl that it probably wasn't smart to be walking through downtown Baltimore. He had just been shot at yesterday in a downtown alley, and his assailant could easily be in one of the vehicles zooming past as he walked toward city hall.

He quickened his pace dramatically and also moved as far from the curb as possible. In no time he was at City Hall Plaza. The security officers in the ornate lobby subjected Darryl to an indifferent security check, as though terrorism could never rear its ugly head in Baltimore.

Darryl was directed toward a suite of third-floor offices. The mayor's personal assistant, Sheila Patterson, was a prim white woman. Darryl guessed that she and the mayor probably had a long-running business relationship.

Darryl idly wondered what it would take to ingratiate himself with Sheila Patterson to the point where she would be willing to spill some of Hudson's dark secrets. She directed Darryl to a waiting area where a walnut coffee table contained a wide variety of reading material, including the most recent edition of *Jet* magazine.

"Well, if it isn't Baltimore's most famous newspaper reporter!"

Darryl turned to see Hizzoner, Charles Hudson, who was nattily dressed in a chocolate brown, double-breasted suit with pinstripes, expensive-looking, brown leather loafers, a white oxford shirt, and a yellow bow tie with brown polka dots.

Hudson's wavy black hair shone so fiercely it appeared to be lacquered to his head. His thick mustache was carefully trimmed so as not to extend past his thin, somewhat feminine-looking lips. Instead of the megawatt smile Hudson was always photographed with, today he wore a pensive-looking, vaguely pained expression.

The other thing that stood out about Baltimore's most powerful politician was that he had a shiner under his left eye. Hudson, or someone, had dabbed pancake makeup on it, but Baltimore's mayor definitely had a black eye!

"I have to stop playing basketball with hackers," Hudson said, pointing to his face and laughing lightly.

Darryl rose and extended his hand. The mayor seemed intent on demonstrating he had the manly grip of a polar bear as he vigorously shook hands with Darryl.

"Come on back to my office, Darryl—do you mind if I call you Darryl?" Hudson asked as he walked through the waiting area toward an oak door with a highly polished, ostentatious brass nameplate: CHARLES V. HUDSON, MAYOR OF BALTIMORE CITY.

"What does the *V* stand for, Mr. Mayor?" Darryl asked, already knowing the answer. He was merely trying to disarm

Hudson, to lower his defenses for the aggressive line of questioning Darryl had planned.

"Oh, that? My great-grandfather on my mother's side was named Vernon," he said easily as he lead Darryl through the doorway to his inner sanctum. "He was from a long line of Hudsons who were merchants in Savannah, Georgia."

Darryl scribbled that tidbit in his notepad before looking up to catalog Hudson's impressive oak-paneled office. It was filled with the typical knickknacks that powerful politicians accumulate—rows of plaques, shelves of books probably signed by their authors, a glass-encased baseball signed by Cal Ripken, et cetera. Darryl took special note of the Harvard undergraduate and Yale law degrees on the walls.

He smiled to himself, thinking he had yet to meet an African-American from Yale Law School who had much common sense.

Sitting behind a massive paper-strewn desk the size of a battleship, Hudson motioned for Darryl to have a seat in front of him.

"My father's family comes from Savannah, too," Darryl said lightly, looking directly into Hudson's tan-colored eyes now. "I come from a long line of Billupses who never plied a legitimate trade."

Hudson gave a tight little laugh. "Oh, that's good, Darryl," he said. Darryl smiled, simultaneously writing the words *smarmy* and *insincere* on his notepad.

"Soooo, what can I do you for, Darryl?" Hudson asked, knowing full well what had occasioned the reporter's visit.

Extracting his microcassette recorder from the pocket of Mad Dawg's sport jacket and praying that a joint or some bit of drug paraphernalia didn't come tumbling out, Darryl set the recorder on the mayor's desk.

"Mind if I turn this on?" he asked easily.

Hudson nodded.

"Mr. Mayor," Darryl said, launching into his interview, "it must have been a tremendous shock for you when the body of your former fiancée was discovered this week."

A look of mild consternation flashed across Hudson's face, as if he had thought they were going to sit down and discuss the weather or something.

"*Surprise* isn't the word for it," Hudson said in a maudlin voice. "I am a happily married man now, but it was still heart-wrenching when Adrienne Jackson's body turned up after all these years. She was a lovely, precious woman, someone who was as warm and personable and loving as she was talented."

Hudson paused, a tear beginning to well up in the corner of his blackened, left eye.

"My heart goes out to Adrienne's family, her friends, and her legions of fans. I know how devastating this is for them, because this is a tremendously distressing development for me also." Inching out of his chair, Hudson pulled a handkerchief from his back pocket and dabbed at his left eye, which remained trained on Darryl's face.

"Out of the thousands of bodies that have been worked on at the medical examiner's office, why do you think Adrienne Jackson's is the only one to have disappeared, Mr. Mayor?"

The grief was gone from Hudson's face now, replaced by what appeared to be outrage. Hudson gestured toward the tape recorder, indicating that he wanted Darryl to turn it off. Darryl complied.

"Let's go off the record for a second here, brother man," Hudson said easily, flashing two perfectly aligned rows of sharp white teeth at Darryl. "Where, exactly, are you going with this? You out to win a Pulitzer, my man?"

Hudson's questions and mannerisms annoyed Darryl. He had little patience for black folks who never seemed conscious of race when things went well but could wrap themselves in a red, black, and green flag fast enough once the shit hit the fan.

He also resented the implication that black journalists are somehow disloyal when they report on black officials and public figures who screw up and do things that hurt the public—including black folks.

"No, I'm definitely not out to win a Pulitzer," Darryl said calmly. "Adrienne Jackson's death and the disappearance of her body have just raised a lot of questions. I'm asking the same questions the man on the street is asking."

"Does the man on the street want to nail me to the cross?" Hudson asked, trying unsuccessfully to inject a note of levity into his voice.

"No, actually there's a lot of sympathy for you out there, Mr. Mayor," Darryl said, surprised that Hudson wasn't making a better show of masking his paranoia. "I'm going to turn this thing on again and go back on the record," Darryl added, pointing to the microcassette recorder on the mayor's desk.

Hudson nodded.

"Mayor Hudson, what kind of person was Adrienne Jackson?"

Hudson had clearly given that question a good deal of thought, for he waxed eloquent for a couple of minutes about Adrienne Jackson's vivacious personality and her dedication to her musical career. The question also relaxed the mayor somewhat, as Darryl had anticipated.

"Mayor Hudson, who would want to take Adrienne Jackson's life?"

"I don't know, Darryl; I really don't know," Hudson quickly replied, dabbing at both eyes now. "She was the kind of person who had no enemies. I will tell you one thing, though—now that she appears to have been murdered, this city's fine homicide detectives will spare no effort to bring her killer, or killers, to justice."

"What do you think happened to your onetime fiancée's body, Mr. Mayor?" Darryl said, rephrasing the question he'd posed earlier.

Hudson's eyes narrowed. Apparently, this Darryl Billups character still hadn't gotten the message. This was supposed to be an easygoing little fluff session where Darryl served up softballs and the mayor hit them out of the park. It was time to shut things down.

"I don't know what could have possibly happened, Darryl, but clearly there's been a massive breakdown in the evidence chain as it relates to Adrienne's case," Hudson said. "My office is working diligently with various city agencies to answer that question, as well as address the other mysteries surrounding the death of my former fiancée."

Adjusting his bow tie, Hudson started to rise from behind his desk, a signal that the interview was over.

"Mr. Mayor," Darryl said, continuing to press forward, "it's been determined that Adrienne Jackson may have been as much as two months pregnant at the time of her death. Was she carrying your child?"

Looking at Darryl icily, Hudson walked around his desk and snapped off Darryl's tape recorder. "I'd love to indulge your penchant for tabloid journalism, but I've got a city to run here," Hudson snapped. Then he opened the door to his oak-paneled office and waved for Darryl to depart.

Gathering up his tape recorder, Darryl stood and slowly walked out the door, writing down Hudson's last statement before it slipped his memory. The mayor smelled lightly of cologne as Darryl passed by him. "Really surprised you would come down here to do a hatchet job on me, *brother*,"

Hudson muttered sarcastically as he closed the door to his office.

Darryl wrote that down, too, guessing he probably wouldn't be on Mayor Hudson's Christmas card list. Then Darryl left city hall for the *Herald*, catching a cab for the return trip. The thought of cars whizzing up the one-way street behind him as he walked along the sidewalk was a little unnerving.

The clean-shaven Middle Eastern cabdriver was clearly disgusted when Darryl gave a destination only four blocks away, but his frown quickly turned upside down when he received a ten-dollar bill and instructions to keep the change. *Money makes the world go round*, Darryl laughed to himself as he bounded up the granite steps leading to the *Baltimore Herald*'s front lobby.

Was money behind the disappearance and death of Hudson's fiancée? Apparently not, because she had been discovered wearing extremely expensive jewelry.

He couldn't put his finger on it, but Darryl was willing to bet Mayor Hudson knew what had happened to Adrienne Jackson. The mayor had been a little too . . . what was the word? Practiced? Smooth? Too calm and accepting for someone who'd just learned that the onetime love of his life had been discovered murdered.

Walking into the *Herald*'s ancient lobby and flashing his ID card at the guard, Darryl continued to think about Hudson. Darryl had always viewed the mayor as oily and slick, despite his Ivy League pedigree. The trick for Darryl was to keep his personal feelings out of the story he had to write.

Darryl stepped into the *Herald*'s rickety 1950s-vintage elevator and pushed the button for the fifth floor. As soon as the door closed, Darryl wriggled out of Mad Dawg's sport jacket, then loosened the knot in his necktie and removed it from around his neck.

The *Herald*'s top reporter considered himself fortunate to be a newspaper journalist, but having to wear suits and ties was one aspect of his job Darryl wasn't really crazy about.

The elevator came to a jerky stop on the fifth floor. Darryl and two other passengers looked at one another with uneasy smiles. The *Herald* was owned by a multibillion-dollar media conglomerate based in Manhattan—couldn't it afford a new elevator for one of its biggest newspaper properties?

When Darryl stopped by the sports department, Mad Dawg was anxiously awaiting his return. He snatched his sport jacket from Darryl and shook it vigorously several times, causing other sports reporters to turn and stare.

"Gotta get that stiffness out," Dawg said loudly as Darryl rolled his eyes. "Can't have you messing with my flow."

"Thanks for the jacket, Dawg."

Grinning, Mad Dawg continued to fiercely shake his jacket before hanging it up in the closet. "So, what did Hudson have to say for himself?"

"There wasn't much he really could say," Darryl replied. "What can you say when a body turns up after eighteen years, is stolen from the medical examiner's office, and turns out to be carrying a fetus that's probably your baby?"

Mad Dawg erupted in a belly laugh. "Hudson always has been a dog," Mad Dawg said, oblivious to the irony in his making that statement. "He's screwing a married teacher in the school where my mom is principal."

Darryl nodded. Hudson's extramarital dalliances were common knowledge among the *Herald*'s reporting staff. "He gave me the righteous indignation routine today and kicked me out of his office."

"Well, at least he's consistent," Mad Dawg observed. "Whenever he gets into a tight spot, all he ever does is lie and deny. Hudson reminds me of that joke about the man whose wife catches him buck naked in their bedroom with another woman. After swearing up and down that nothing is going on, the man asks his wife, 'Who you gonna believe—me or your lying eyes?' "

Darryl laughed, picturing a "Don't Believe Your Lying Eyes" headline on the story he was about to write about Hudson and the Safe&Sound case.

Remembering that he had a quasi date with Thelma Holmes that evening, Darryl was able to talk Mad Dawg out of his sport jacket again. Without telling Dawg why he needed it, too, because Dawg sometimes fell victim to diarrhea of the mouth.

Dropping his tape recorder into the breast pocket of Dawg's jacket, Darryl left the sports department and made his way to the newsroom.

NOT SURE WHETHER TO BE flattered or disgusted, Darryl tried to ignore the toothless hag at the next table, who was slurping whiskey from a shot glass and trying desperately to catch his eye. As if that weren't gross enough, a cigarette that seemed to have a foot of ash dangled precariously from her lips.

Cigarette smoke was the predominant smell at the Kit-Kat Club, along with the aroma of stale beer and a faint dried-urine odor that wafted through the establishment every time the men's room door creaked opened.

Why in the world had he invited Thelma Holmes to this godforsaken place? It was dirty, seemed to be stuck in a 1970s time warp, and must have contained most of the black old-head heroin friends and alcoholics in the city.

An old-fashioned coin-operated jukebox was playing the fifth Isley Brothers song to rumble through the club in the last hour, "Fight the Power." Actually, the chest-thumping volume was a good thing, because it prevented Darryl from hearing a single word his toothless pursuer was mouthing in his direction.

"If you're asking if I've seen your dentures, no, I haven't!" Darryl muttered into his beer glass, which had a faint plum-colored lipstick stain on the rim. Now his not-so-secret admirer, who appeared to be in her midfifties, was suggestively licking her shot glass and bending over to give Darryl a glimpse of breasts sagging forlornly inside a low-cut black dress.

All the while she wriggled her behind to the thumping beat of the music, transported back to her glory days by the driving power of the Isleys. Darryl happened to like "Fight the Power" and ordinarily would have been bobbing his head to it. Tonight, though, that might be misconstrued as an invitation to talk, to dance, to . . . ugh!

So Darryl remained stock-still, staring into the bottom of his dirty beer glass, which he had no further interest in drinking from. He sat facing the door, which seemed like a good idea in light of the fact that someone in Baltimore didn't seem terribly fond of him at the moment. Even though he was about to be joined by a cop, a little voice kept murmuring that traveling to the Kit-Kat Club might not have been the most brilliant idea.

Located near North and Pennsylvania Avenues, in a black section of the city where top-notch black businesses and entertainment establishments had prospered prior to desegregation, the Kit-Kat had seen its best times many a decade ago, much like the lonely woman at the next table.

Of the thirty or so patrons present, most of them had turned to glance at Darryl when he entered. His relative youth and trim physique equaled one thing—Five Oh was in the joint and looking to roust someone. Even the bartender, a balding man with gray hair and the thick arms and sturdy back of a stevedore, had sniffed suspiciously when he entered the establishment.

"Somebody named Mr. Greg a regular here?" Darryl had asked.

The old man never stopped stirring his rum and Coke, nor did he look directly at Darryl. "Who wanna know? You gotta warrant?"

Darryl laughed. "No, I don't have a warrant, but I need to talk to him."

"Don't know no Gregory." The man shrugged, snagging a thirty-five-cent tip from the bar. "Sorry."

That surprised Darryl, who had assumed that an old-time barkeep would be more adept at lying than this guy. So he ordered a cheap domestic brew and sat down to wait for Thelma Holmes, as the old girl at the next table repeatedly assaulted him with her eyes. Darryl arrived at the Kit-Kat at 9:45 P.M., fifteen minutes before his "date" with Thelma.

He should never have mixed business and pleasure like this. The journey to the Kit-Kat was all about his fascination with Alonzo Ellis. Baltimore was full of young brothers who had stolen cars or done some shoplifting. Even Darryl had stolen candy once or twice as a boy.

However, making the leap from that kind of stuff to shooting at cops with a .22-caliber just didn't follow. This Greg character who occasionally interacted with Alonzo just might hold the answer to that riddle.

Alonzo was clearly out of his depth, Darryl mused. Why else would he be trying to cap someone with a puny .22-caliber handgun? At the same time, someone else at the scene had been firing a 9mm handgun that killed Adele Jones and Joseph Dennis. That fact had been revealed to Darryl by a police department source.

Darryl looked up just in time to see Thelma Holmes moving

tentatively through the billowing clouds of cigarette smoke inside the club, looking as much a fish out of water as he had a few minutes earlier. She wore a beige pantsuit, brown shoes with flat soles, and a pastel-blue blouse. A small brown purse was snuggled under her arm.

Walking around with a purse in the vicinity of North and Pennsylvania wasn't a great idea. Unless, of course, you happened to be an undercover cop toting a concealed handgun.

Darryl immediately noticed two things about Thelma, one being that the clothes she had on tonight were classier, more stylish, than yesterday's. She looked more like a prosperous businesswoman than a police detective.

The second thing was that she hadn't been wearing makeup yesterday or when he'd unexpectedly dropped by her house, but tonight she had on a modest shade of red lipstick, along with a touch of blue eyeliner. Thelma wasn't a cute woman, as he'd thought yesterday. She was beautiful.

Darryl realized she probably avoided makeup while working in order to keep the focus off her looks. For some reason, he felt a pang of sympathy for her, as if having a stunning appearance was something to be pitied for. However, Darryl had worked around cops long enough to keenly appreciate how chauvinistic and juvenile many of them often could be.

So he guessed that being attractive definitely wasn't a plus for Thelma while on duty.

Darryl popped up from his seat like a jack-in-the-box, glad that Thelma had actually shown up and was eager to slip the aggressive crone at the next table. Thelma spotted him immediately and gave a shy, embarrassed half smile.

She's probably given this some thought and thinks it's as crazy as I do!

They met halfway and Darryl reached for her hand. Against his, it felt soft and smooth. And cool. How did the old wives' tale go—cold hands make for a warm heart?

"Well, this ain't exactly the classiest joint in the city, but I'm glad you could make it," Darryl said, noticing that Thelma had ditched the white gauze bandage on her damaged right ear in favor of a flesh-colored Band-Aid.

"This one of your regular haunts?" Thelma asked quizzically, discreetly taking in her surroundings. Darryl noticed that she quickly cataloged everybody in the Kit-Kat, as well as all of the exits. Good cops maintain situational awareness out of habit.

"I don't usually come here," Darryl said, ushering her toward his table, "but I wanted our first meeting to be memorable." Thelma looked at him oddly, as if unsure whether to laugh or flee. She went directly for Darryl's seat and demurely sat down.

Darryl grabbed the chair on the other side of the table and slid it beside Thelma. "Wouldn't be a good idea to have my back to the door after getting shot at yesterday," he said.

At the next table, Madame Black Dress snorted and threw back her head before wobbling off to the other side of the club.

Thelma turned to Darryl and looked him up and down. "You're not the Kit-Kat type," she said bluntly. "What gives?"

Darryl laughed, more at her directness than anything. "Well, I'm a smoker," he lied. "Instead of smoking one cigarette at a time, I can come here for ten minutes, breathe in a couple of packs, then leave."

Thelma chuckled and rolled her eyes. "Corny, Darryl," she said with a smile, "although the smoke in this place will ruin my clothes if I stay much longer. Seriously, what's up?"

Darryl took a moment to contemplate his answer before he responded. "Seriously, I owe you an apology. My visit here is work-related and I should never have invited you to join me. What do you say we split and go someplace nice?"

As Darryl rose from his chair, the muscular old bartender

came from behind the bar and made his way toward Darryl, gimping along on two arthritic knees. He reminded Darryl of a lurching ship, suddenly looming out of the fog as he made his way through the clouds of cigarette smoke blanketing the inside of the Kit-Kat. Grandly brandishing a tarnished silver serving tray holding two glasses of champagne, he stopped directly in front of Darryl.

"Young blood, I owes you an apology," the bartender said in a raspy voice. "I ain't tryin' to be rude, but narcs been here all week messin' with my customers." He thrust the champagne glasses toward Darryl and Thelma. "On the Kit-Kat Club, folks. Sorry."

Thelma shrugged and shot the bartender a wan smile. She and Darryl both would have preferred not to spend another second in the Kit-Kat, but neither wanted to insult an elder bearing gifts.

"Can't hurt, I guess," Thelma said, sliding comically back into her seat.

Darryl slunk down glumly beside her. "Thank you, sir," he said, averting his gaze from the bartender's eyes. "That was thoughtful."

The champagne glasses were placed in front of Darryl and Thelma and the bartender cleared his throat to unleash a toast.

"You two lookin' good together," the bartender said simply. Thelma stifled a laugh, clinked her glass against Darryl's, and quickly turned it bottom-up. Darryl followed suit so they could finally leave the Kit-Kat and get the evening properly under way.

The old bartender smiled kindly. "Yeah, them cops rude, I tell ya," he said, removing the champagne glasses from the table and stooping so that he was eye level with Darryl and Thelma. "Not very nice peoples. I is so sorrry."

Darryl looked directly at the old man, who appeared to be hobbling a lot more than he was a few seconds ago and had also begun to slur his words dramatically. Alarmed that the gentleman could be suffering a stroke, Darryl stood up to help the man steady himself. But when he rose, the room began to gyrate in the same manner as the bartender.

The Kit-Kat's clientele were starting to slide about in their chairs, as though on the deck of a wildly rolling ocean-liner. Disoriented, Darryl sank to his knees and squeezed his eyes shut.

Warm liquid hit the front of his shirt, as well as the sport jacket he'd borrowed from Mad Dawg—those winos were shaking the ship to the point where the ocean was splashing against the sides of the boat and drenching Darryl. A sudden urge to sleep gripped him. He fought it, irrationally fearing that if he surrendered to sleep, death would be right on its heels.

Darryl's eyes fluttered open long enough to see the bartender hovering over him, looking serene and unsurprised.

Where was Thelma? Darryl tried unsuccessfully to call out to her. His mouth and nose burned fiercely.

I can't breathe; I can't breathe—oh my God!

The lights behind the bar grew dimmer and dimmer until blackness enveloped Darryl. The sensation reminded him of the time when he was a little boy playing in the Atlantic Ocean at Cape May, New Jersey, and an unusually high wave came along and knocked him down, then sucked him under the water. It seemed that the harder he fought, the deeper he was drawn into the water, until finally he felt the strong, rough hands of his father yanking him toward the surface and life-giving air.

Darryl was feeling the same sense of terror and helplessness now. Only this time, his father was nowhere to be found.

Finally realizing that his effort to remain conscious would be as difficult as trying to defeat gravity, Darryl surrendered himself to blackness.

The Isley Brothers stopped singing one by one, their voices shutting down first, then their instruments, leaving the Kit-Kat Club deathly quiet.

CHAPTER 16

The first sound Darryl heard when he awoke was a chortle. A deep-voiced, rolling guffaw bursting forth from someone tickled to death about something. As loud as the laughter was, though, it was joyless. Rather, it was the mean-sounding laugh of someone who'd finally outwitted or out-maneuvered a longtime foe, the chortle of someone who was thrilled to be in a position to exact revenge. Or get the final word. The effect was chilling.

"'Retribution is mine, sayeth the Lord,'" Darryl mumbled groggily, prompting a whole new spate of laughter.

"Shit—if that the case, open yo' eyes and meet the Lord, muthafucka!" a baritone voice boomed somewhere over Darryl's head. A strong odor of cologne was in the air. The same cologne Darryl had sniffed in Mayor Hudson's office, but twice as strong. The aroma sent uncontrollable spasms of nausea rolling through Darryl's stomach and he began to retch, unable to catch his breath. The contents of his stomach had been expelled hours ago, along with whatever had been slipped into his champagne glass at the Kit-Kat Club. Opening his right eye ever so slowly, Darryl saw a narrow horizontal beam of light.

Darryl realized he was lying on a hard, level surface of some sort.

"Where's Thelma?" Darryl grunted. It took quite a bit of energy to convert his thoughts into words.

"You mean da bitch who shot my boy, Zo? Right beside you," the deep voice said, vibrating with contempt.

That made no sense whatsoever to Darryl's slow-moving brain. The only "Zo" it was familiar with was star basketball player Alonzo Mourning . . . unless the voice was talking about . . . Alonzo Ellis.

It was gradually dawning on Darryl what was taking place. The more information his mind began to process, the more desperate he felt.

"You must be Mr. Greg," he blurted, praying that a denial would follow.

"In da flesh, newspaper boy!" the voice boomed.

Forcing both eyes open, Darryl could see that he was in a dimly lit place and that someone was hovering over him. He was in no condition to put any weight on his legs and couldn't feel his hands, which were behind him. In addition to cologne, the smell of vomit hung heavy in the air.

The odor was overpowering—Darryl realized it was his and could feel wetness on the front of his shirt. Mad Dawg's sport coat must have been a wreck.

Moaning began to fill the darkened room or enclosure where Darryl was. It was a female voice that sounded disoriented and angry.

"Stop trying to undo your hands, bitch!" Darryl heard a thumping sound, like someone being struck in the chest, and Thelma's voice rose several octaves as she cried out in pain.

"You okay, Thelma?" Darryl asked, his voice sounding incredibly loud in the darkness. A boot struck with tremendous force on the tip of Darryl's tailbone, and he yelled out in surprise as much as in pain.

"Damned stupid of y'all to come looking for me at the Kit-Kat," Gregory said in a sneering voice. "Y'all dumb mutha-fuckas didn't know I owned the joint?"

"No, I didn't know," Darryl said quietly. That blow to his tailbone managed to sweep quite a few cobwebs from his head. Now he could see that the horizontal strip of light was really a ray of sunlight streaming under a closed door. Darryl lay about five feet away from the door.

His tormentor stood directly behind him, probably ready to deliver another jolting blow with his boot. Moving his right leg slowly, Darryl found that his legs were loosely bound. But his wrists were tightly encircled, cutting off the circulation to his hands.

"She didn't come looking for you," Darryl said, tasting tremendously bitter and nasty vomit residue in his mouth. "I was the one who was looking for you. Why don't you let her go?—your beef is with me."

" 'Why don't you let her go?' " Gregory said in a mocking tone. Darryl grunted as a boot smacked into his right shoulder blade, blasting air from his lungs. "Let her go so she can call her cop friends? Don't think so, newspaper boy."

Several minutes passed in silence. Darryl could just barely hear Thelma and Gregory breathing over the sound of blood rushing through his ears, which nearly drowned out everything.

"You know you've got a Baltimore City cop, right?" Thelma said angrily. "They're gonna be looking for me."

Gregory chuckled lightly. "Nobody lookin' for yo' asses," he scoffed. "Nobody would ever look *here*."

Gregory seemed so absolutely certain of that that Darryl's heart sank. Where the hell was here? Trying to rein in his wildly galloping heart, Darryl strained to listen. He hoped to hear a distinctive noise or two that might give their location away. The sound of traffic, the burbling of a brook, the noise of an airplane taking off nearby.

But all he heard was silence. Where could you go in Baltimore to achieve total silence? Druid Hill Park was one possibility. Another was that they were in a suburban setting. None of the hubbub of the city could be heard—not the barking of a dog or the sounds of children playing.

A more immediate concern began to throb in Darryl's mind—he had to use the bathroom in the worst possible way. Not only did he have to pee, but whatever had been used to knock him out had upset his stomach terribly.

"Can I please use the bathroom?" Thelma said plaintively as if reading Darryl's mind.

"Hell, naw. Go where you is—don't make no difference." Neither Darryl nor Thelma said anything after that, thinking the same thought. Darryl calmly mused that if he had to die, he would like to tell his mother that he loved her one final time. And he thought about how frugal he'd always been and how he'd always dreamed of driving a race car but had been too afraid to try.

He would donate more to charity and would race cars every weekend if only God would grant him a second chance. Because he wasn't ready to die. He wasn't afraid of death—he just didn't want to go now, and like this.

Stop thinking about dying, Darryl. Concentrate on what you can do to keep living.

So Darryl began to focus in on his abductor. He was a

powerful, muscular man, judging from his deep voice and from the power with which he'd kicked Darryl in the back. He was clearly angry, partially about Alonzo. What else, God only knew.

Instead of initiating more conversation, Darryl planned to let Mr. Greg do all the talking. That might allow Darryl to pick up some more clues on this violent man's mind-set. And might provide an opening for Darryl to talk his way out of this mess.

"Whatcha shoot Zo for, whore?" Gregory asked quietly. Darryl noted the change in his voice and demeanor when the conversation shifted to Alonzo Ellis.

"Because he was firing a gun at me," Thelma said forcefully. "I had to defend myself, and I did."

"Didn't make no difference he was a kid, huh?"

Thelma didn't answer.

"You ain't the law no more," Gregory said. "I'm the damn law, now. And when I ax you somethin'"—Darryl heard a boot slam into Thelma's midsection, unleashing a geyser of air from her nostril—"you answer. Got that?"

Darryl wanted to jump up and beat the hell out of Gregory. But given that he wasn't exactly dealing from a position of strength, said nothing.

"I see . . . nothing has changed . . . eh, Greg?" Thelma said, wheezing as she struggled to breathe. "You always were a bully . . . and a coward . . . *Gregory Hudson!*"

"How you know that? What make you think that my name?" Gregory asked quickly. Darryl wanted to know, too, curious how Thelma had come up with that information.

"Don't worry about that," Thelma said, still wheezing slightly. "All you need to know is that the police know about you. And Adrienne is watching everything you're doing here, so you need to get yourself in check."

Stunned, Gregory staggered toward the back of the room, away from the doorway. Darryl listened to the exchange between his fellow prisoner and their captor in amazement.

"How you know that?" Gregory roared, his voice suddenly so agitated that Darryl was instantly alarmed. He quietly flexed his legs, testing the tightness of his bonds. Darryl guessed that Thelma's legs were restrained, too.

"I have powers you can't begin to imagine," Thelma said mysteriously. "You really need to set me and Darryl free."

Gregory made no effort to release his captives, nor did he leave the back of the room. Darryl didn't know what Thelma was up to, but she had clearly done a number on Gregory's head. Darryl could practically hear the wheels turning.

Twenty minutes passed with Gregory continuing to lurk silently in the quiet, dark room.

"Turn yourself in, Gregory," Thelma said in a soothing voice. "That's what Adrienne would want."

"*Shut up!*" Gregory exploded. "Stop using that fuckin' name. Do it again and I swear I'll blow both of you away."

"Oughta just get that gas can outta my trunk and burn your asses up," Gregory muttered, thinking aloud.

"Like you did to my house?" Darryl asked. He knew he was risking another blow, but he had to know.

"Right, like I did to your house, punk," Gregory said malevolently. "Your car, too. Reporters supposed to be smart?" A loud cough erupted in the darkness, followed by the roar of someone clearing his throat. Gregory made a spitting sound and Darryl heard a glob of mucus splatter on the floor inches from his head.

It was clear that Darryl and Thelma were to be humiliated and shorn of every vestige of dignity before meeting their final fate. Whatever that was.

"You shot at me from the alley, too, didn't you?"

"Damn skippy. Gettin' rusty, I guess."

Darryl heard a scratching noise, like a mouse or squirrel rubbing its claws on wood, followed by the flickering light of a match that lasted inside the room for a few seconds before it went out. There had been enough time for Darryl to see that he was surrounded by white, windowless cinder-block walls. He guessed he was in a basement of some kind. The smell of cigarette smoke wafted his way. Darryl prayed a cigarette would calm Gregory, remove some of his violent edge.

As Gregory huffed and puffed on his cigarette, Darryl wondered if Thelma was wearing an ankle holster under her pantsuit. Not that it would be of any use if her hands and legs were bound.

Gregory was on the move now—that was easy to ascertain from the clodhopper footsteps that resonated through the floor and set it vibrating. The slow, unhurried footsteps moved from the rear of the room to a point directly behind Darryl. He braced, expecting another kick.

But this time the blow was to his eyes, in the form of a brilliant ceiling light that suddenly flooded the cinder-block room where he and Thelma were being held prisoner. Darryl looked up at Gregory, a huge, handsome black man wearing fashionably tight, faded blue jeans, a green polo shirt stretched across a heavily muscled chest, and pointed-toe black cowboy boots made of alligator.

"Whatcha starin' at, newspaper boy? You gay or somethin'?"

Darryl looked away and, with tremendous difficulty, managed to pivot his body around on the floor to look at Thelma.

She was lying on her side with her back to the far wall. The front of her blouse was stained with dried vomit, and her pants were also wet from her having relieved herself.

You would have thought she was in the catbird seat, though, judging from the defiant glare she shot at Gregory. It was a look you'd want to see on the GI next to you as the two of you hunkered down in a foxhole, waiting to go into battle.

Darryl and Thelma were spoiling for an opportunity to take Gregory out. There was almost a palpable sense of quiet resistance in the air. Neither the reporter nor the cop planned to go quietly into that good night.

The only question was: How could they possibly resist? Darryl already had some ideas.

By now, Darryl's bladder had gone from being merely uncomfortable to an ocean-toting, screaming banshee. Rather than ask to relieve himself again, Darryl stubbornly fought off the urge. There was no way he would have Thelma see him wet his pants. Here he was, a possible heartbeat or two away from death, worrying about appearances in front of some woman he hardly knew.

Teeth clenched, Darryl tried to visualize arid deserts, dried-up riverbeds, any other mental picture bereft of moisture. He strained to the point that he began to quiver with exertion.

But the human body was designed to excrete waste products, not retain them. A warm cascade eventually began to flow down the front of Darryl's slacks, pooling on the floor near his midsection.

Naturally Darryl said nothing, hoping his accident would go unnoticed. However, Gregory had observed something glistening on the floor and took immediate steps to compound this latest indignity.

"Nasty little pisspot!"

Darryl felt a kick much harder than the first two explode into his left kidney. Gritting his teeth, he exhaled sharply and arched his back. He wasn't prepared for the follow-up kick that scored a bull's-eye on his spine and left him writhing in pain.

Spikes of pain radiated throughout Darryl's back, into his

chest cavity, and through the back of his thighs. It was clear that he and Thelma would need to move quickly.

Apparently satisfied that he'd done enough damage for the time being, Gregory abruptly snapped off the bare light-bulb hanging from the ceiling.

Darryl had already committed his prison cell to memory before the light went off. They appeared to be in the basement of an older building, judging from the construction and condition of the wooden supports in the ceiling.

The floor was made of wooden slats, a fraction of an inch between each one, and there appeared to be a hole in the floor created by a rat or some other rodent. Darryl elected not to mention this to Thelma once Gregory was gone.

The door to their prison was made of old, sturdily built wood and secured by at least two massive black locks.

One other thing Darryl noticed before the light was extinguished and the room again turned mostly dark—Thelma's hands were tightly bound, but her legs were barely tied at all.

With the silent menace of a shark gliding around its prey, Gregory wordlessly opened the door to the room holding his prisoners and slammed it shut. That was followed by the metal-on-metal sound of a sliding dead bolt, followed by the noise of a key activating the tumblers to a lock and the sound of another lock snapping into place.

Sensing that Gregory was just outside the door, Darryl kept quiet. Sure enough, after a moment, Gregory's boots could be heard pounding up a set of steps—Darryl counted twenty-four footsteps. Then a door squeaked open and shut and another lock turned.

"What do you think he's up to?" Darryl asked in a whisper that sounded like a shout in the still room.

"Don't have a clue," Thelma whispered back. "But I can guarantee we won't like it."

Darryl wondered how long he could survive being

Gregory's personal soccer ball, but he didn't share that with Thelma. Every conversation they had in this hellish place needed to be upbeat and optimistic.

"We need to wriggle across the floor so we can put our backs together," Darryl said. "Then maybe you can move your fingers enough to untie my hands. My stuff is so tight I can't even feel my hands—otherwise, I'd untie you first."

"Sssshhhh! Listen."

Somebody was walking around upstairs, splashing something on the floor above Darryl and Thelma. The person moved about methodically, tossing liquid as he went. A few drops of whatever was being splashed leaked through the ceiling and spattered onto the floor between Darryl and Thelma.

A familiar, pungent odor pierced the air—*gasoline*.

Both were terrified of hearing the *Whoooosh!* that would signify an inferno was under way. Darryl started wriggling furiously across the rough wooden floor, picking up scores of splinters in the process.

His quest was to somehow get his hands free before a fire started. He and Thelma might still die, but at least their hands would be free. Giving them a shot at kicking down the wooden door.

Darryl had squirmed about ten feet when he felt Thelma's legs against his back. She had managed to force the loosely looped plastic rope that constrained her legs far enough apart that both of her feet had a few inches of movement.

That allowed her to slink across the dirty wooden floor at a much faster pace than Darryl.

Like Darryl, Thelma had also become a veritable pincushion filled with wood splinters.

The only sensation she was conscious of, however, was the strong odor of gasoline. She was certain of two things—Gregory Hudson had murdered Adrienne Jackson, and he would not balk at turning her and Darryl into crispy critters.

More gasoline was starting to rain down into what might be Darryl and Thelma's death chamber, if they didn't do something quickly. They maneuvered into a position where their backs were flush, allowing their hands to touch.

"I can't feel my hands at all," Darryl said in a tight-sounding voice. "What about you?"

"A little feeling in the right one," Thelma grunted. "I can feel the knot in the rope around your wrist."

Darryl stiffened suddenly. "What is *that*?" he hissed. Several tinkling little musical tones rang out, tones one might expect to hear from an ice-cream truck trying to lure little children.

The notes stopped suddenly, followed by a voice instantly recognizable as Gregory's. "Yeah? . . . Uh-huh, uh-huh. . . . Naw, I got 'em in the spot we talked 'bout. 'Bout to burn their asses up right now."

Then Gregory was silent, taking in whatever the person at the other end of the phone had to say. "What the fuck else we gonna do with 'em?" he spit out, sounding dejected. "Okay. We gonna have to ice 'em at some point, though. Later."

The sound of a bouncing metal gasoline can thundered across the ceiling over Darryl's and Thelma's heads, followed by heavy footsteps moving slowly across the floor—Darryl was too scared to count the number this time. The footsteps stopped; then a door opened and slammed shut, vibrating throughout the foundation of the building.

A car started somewhere outside—Darryl could tell from the engine note that it was a high-performance V-8—and pulled away. The vehicle had a stick-shift transmission, Darryl noted, listening with relief as the exhaust note grew more and more distant until finally, mercifully, it disappeared.

Thelma released a huge sigh. "Thank God." Darryl said nothing. "Do you hear that, Darryl?" Another presence was in the room with them, an animal whose clawed feet could clearly be heard scampering across the slats of the floor. Whatever it was, it sounded like it was a few feet away and had probably been stirred by the gasoline dripping onto the floor.

"No, I don't hear a thing," Darryl lied. "Keep working at that knot." The little clawed feet stopped moving when Darryl spoke and stayed silent for a couple of minutes. Then Darryl heard them again, walking behind him. Meaning that whatever it was happened to be closer to Thelma, whose right hand began to move frantically with the approach of their guest.

"Slow down, Thelma," Darryl said in a reassuring voice. "Everything's cool—just take your time and get it right." The not-so-tiny footsteps were quiet once again, then boldly resumed. The animal began scampering about the room, moving in the direction of Darryl's and Thelma's heads.

It was giving them wide berth, whatever it was, Darryl observed gratefully. He kept his eyes on the slit of light creeping under the door. If the mystery guest went past it, the resulting silhouette should allow Darryl to identify it.

"What's that perfume you have on?" Darryl said suddenly, partially to break the tension and partially to keep Thelma's mind—not to mention his own—off the scurrying varmint.

"Feels like a gorilla tied this knot," Thelma growled, ignoring the comment. "I can only get like two or three fingers on it at a time."

"We'll get out of this rope," Darryl said confidently, a statement made solely for his benefit. That's what he had to believe and strive for with every fiber of his being.

As Thelma continued grappling with the bindings around his wrist, hurling a quiet curse word every now and then, the creature finally crawled in front of the door. Judging from the outline that slowly materialized, it was either a small cat with an incredibly narrow head and huge buck teeth or the biggest rat Darryl had ever laid eyes on.

It turned its head toward Darryl, and he could see sparkles of light coming off the creature's whiskers. Goose bumps rose on Darryl's body from head to toe—he was totally at this thing's mercy.

"How's it coming, Thelma?" he asked anxiously.

"No looser than when I started," she replied matter-of-factly. "And I have to go to the bathroom like nobody's business."

"Your stomach, too?"

"God almighty, yes. Please excuse me in advance for anything you might hear."

"That goes double for me," Darryl said, noting that the sharp-toothed animal near the door was slowly advancing. He could see its ugly little rat feet and its characteristic herky-jerky rodent movements.

The animal would wreak havoc on Darryl's face and probably gnaw out his eyes if it got an opportunity. No longer creeping now, the rat was jogging directly toward Darryl's head.

Raising his head off the floor, Darryl opened his mouth as wide as humanly possible and summoned every negative, repellent vibe he could muster.

"*Noooooooooooooo!*" Darryl angrily bellowed as loud as he could. Thelma stiffened, and her hand stopped moving against his wrist.

The noise and the quick upward movement of Darryl's head sent the animal scurrying, back into the hole in the floor Darryl hoped. He felt light-headed from forcing so much oxygen from his lungs and from the pervasive smell of gasoline inside the makeshift dungeon.

"A rat, right?" Thelma asked unemotionally.

"Not just any rat, superrat," Darryl replied disgustedly.

"That's what I thought. You don't have to sugarcoat stuff, Darryl. Just give it to me straight. I'm a big girl."

Darryl said nothing, listening for the return of their friend. Rats tend to be fearless, persistent, vicious little things. "All right, here's the world as I see it, Thelma," he said after a while. "The next time Gregory sticks his fat head in this place, we need to be in a position to kill or cripple him."

"We're on the same page, brother," Thelma said, starting to work on Darryl's plastic handcuffs once again. The little line of light under the door slowly turned golden, then red, then existed no more. The room was pitch-black.

Under those conditions, the touch of another human being was definitely reassuring. Especially a levelheaded brother who appeared to be able to handle his business, Thelma thought as she doggedly picked away at the knotted plastic rope wrapped around Darryl's wrist.

Even though it was dark, she could tell that the nail on her right index finger was broken, partially ripped, and bleeding like mad. With any luck, the overpowering smell of gasoline would keep the rat from getting the scent of blood.

The gas odor made Thelma think about liquids, which in turn made her think about how incredibly thirsty she was. The last thing she or Darryl had had to drink was that champagne someone had slipped a mickey into. The chloral hydrate had totally sapped her and Darryl's appetites, however, so neither one of them was hungry.

Every now and then they would hear the rat scurrying around under the floor's wooden slats. Darryl and Thelma would take a few seconds to scream and bang their feet on the floor.

After a while, Thelma had pushed the overworked muscles and tendons in her frazzled right hand well past the limits of human endurance. The rope around Darryl's wrists appeared no closer to giving up its grip, but Thelma had no choice but to give her aching hand a second or two to rest.

"How in the world did you know that guy's name?" Darryl asked admiringly.

Thelma slowly opened and closed her right hand, trying to get blood circulating through the abused appendage. "To be honest, I had no clue until I talked to my mother this morning," she said modestly. "She couldn't believe it when she heard the Safe&Sound victim resembled Adrienne Jackson. Adrienne was my mom's first cousin and they used to talk all the time . . . about really private stuff.

"When Adrienne disappeared, she was engaged and seeing another man on the side. That man was Gregory Hudson." Thelma flexed her hand faster now, feeling some of the strength return. "When you said 'Mr. Greg,' I just took a stab in the dark that it was Gregory Hudson," she said triumphantly.

"Damn good guess," Darryl conceded. "Adrienne was engaged to Mayor Hudson, right?"

Thelma laughed as if Darryl were pulling her leg. "Why, of course. How did you know that?"

"I did a little research in the *Herald*'s library last night," Darryl said. "I was in Mayor Hudson's office this morning— he kicked me out when I started asking about Adrienne's fetus."

Now it was Thelma's turn to pick Darryl's brain, before attacking his bindings once again. "How did you know about the fetus?" she said. "Even I didn't know about that."

"It was easy," Darryl replied. "A source in the medical examiner's office."

"Sssshhhh! What's that?" Thelma asked, her voice suddenly fearful.

Darryl didn't know what she was talking about at first. Then he heard a faint droning sound grow louder and louder, turning into a basso profundo rumble. The rumble of a powerful American V-8 engine. Darryl cringed inwardly, hoping the vehicle kept going past wherever they were.

Thelma started pulling frantically at the rope around Darryl's wrists—it felt like a piece of clothesline.

The rumbling automobile slowed its pace, stopping nearby. Then the driver revved the engine one time and cut it. Darryl definitely didn't want to be tied up and prostrate the next time Gregory returned. *But things don't always turn out the way we hope, do they?* Darryl thought, feeling a bit of defeatism slip into his psyche.

As much as he didn't want to entertain the thought, Darryl couldn't help but envision the maniacal Gregory striding toward the building in his cowboy boots, smiling as he toted a fresh book of matches.

Without exchanging a word, Darryl and Thelma began to roll across the unfinished wooden floor, impaling their backs, stomachs, legs, and arms with even more splinters in their haste to separate before Gregory came back downstairs.

Provided he didn't simply flick a match into the upstairs section and keep going.

There was a tremendous amount of fumbling upstairs, at the door to the building, before it opened. The heavy footsteps that entered didn't sound nearly as steady as the ones that had departed. Now they occasionally stumbled and stutter-stepped.

"Sounds like he went to the bar," Darryl whispered.

The footsteps crossed the ceiling and the glow of an electric lightbulb shone under the door. Then someone very slowly and cautiously began to descend the stairs. Darryl counted twenty-one steps before whomever it was rumbled down the last three with a tremendous racket.

"Shit!" Immediately afterward, rustling could be heard outside the door to the room. Alas, Gregory appeared to be alive and well. If the sober Gregory was a sadistic, heartless fuck, what kind of unspeakable monster would the inebriated Gregory be? Darryl and Thelma would find out soon enough.

Someone inserted a key into the door with great difficulty before the distinct sound of the tumblers engaging could be heard. Followed by the metal-on-metal sound of the dead bolt sliding open.

"Don't y'all try nothin' stooopid now," Gregory slurred as he entered the room, followed by wonderful rays of light. He somehow managed to step over Darryl and flicked on the bare lightbulb. A superstrong odor of gasoline followed Gregory into the room.

"What y'all been doin' down here?" Gregory growled, glancing at Darryl and Thelma as if surprised to see they hadn't moved.

Darryl squinted up at Gregory, his eyes not used to the sudden harsh light. *We've been partying hearty down here, dumb ass. What the hell did you think?*

Darryl just lay on the floor, looking at Gregory as if he had climbed out of the primate house at Baltimore's zoo. Gregory was puffing contentedly on a little brown cigarillo, in spite of all the gasoline fumes circulating inside the building. Darryl started to say something, but bringing up the subject might remind the beast of why he had flung gas throughout the house in the first place.

"There's a rat down here—can you do something about it . . . please?" Darryl was shocked to hear anything remotely civil come out of Thelma's mouth. What was she up to?

"Where?"

Thelma looked toward the hole in the floor where the creature had entered. Walking unsteadily, Gregory got down on one knee and peered into the hole, as if the rodent were conveniently standing there, waiting to exchange greetings. Taking a drag on his cigarillo, Gregory blew a mighty lungful of light blue smoke into the hole.

When nothing happened, he carefully stood up, his head mere inches from the low ceiling. He gazed around, a warden taking in the contents of a prison cell. Darryl received a casual, indifferent glance, and he returned a stare conveying an equal measure of warmth and affection.

When Gregory's eyes took in Thelma and her pitiful plight, however, he stared at her for several seconds.

Darryl could only guess what was going through the man's tiny brain.

"What a cute girl like you wanna be a cop for?" he asked, genuinely puzzled. As if the highest goal an attractive female could strive for was to be a giggly bimbo on some player's arm. Darryl was proud of Thelma when she simply ignored Gregory. The defiant action was in keeping with this tough, fiercely proud woman's personality.

"Don't y'all go nowhere!" Gregory muttered with a short laugh as he ambled out of the room. There were no footsteps on the stairs this time, just the sound of Gregory fumbling around in the basement. Just outside the door Darryl could see an old oil-fired furnace but little else.

His view was blocked when Gregory came back through the doorway, carrying something in his huge right fist.

Gregory returned to the hole where the rat was hiding and dropped something into it.

"What's that?" Thelma asked in a hard voice.

"Rat poison," Gregory said. His voice was bursting with pride, as though he'd accomplished some honorable deed meriting a pat on the back.

Darryl marveled at his captor's behavior. Instead of being a mean drunk, Gregory actually allowed little kernels of compassion to bubble to the surface. It was generally the other way around with most drinkers. Maybe because Gregory was such a volatile, miserable bastard ordinarily, it took alcohol to pry loose the decent side of his personality. Darryl and Thelma would have to try to get Gregory even drunker at some point.

"Man, we haven't had any water all day," Darryl said suddenly. "Can we have some water, please?"

Instead of cussing or ridiculing Darryl's request, Gregory sighed. "Have to untie your hands fo' that," he said. "Maybe tomorrow." He continued to peer into the rat hole, undoubtedly upset at the thought of bringing a kindred spirit to an untimely end, Darryl mused.

Gregory stood upright again and took another long look at Thelma before walking to the center of the room to turn off the light. Each of his plodding steps sent vibrations through the wooden floor that jostled Darryl and Thelma.

"The mayor knows we're here, doesn't he?" Darryl said with certainty just as Gregory's hand was reaching toward the ceiling to cut off the light. Gregory paused, and Darryl flinched inside, not sure if a fusillade of kicks was about to rain down on his head and back.

"He know you here," Gregory finally said, snapping off the light. "That the only reason yo' asses ain't dead now." So much for alcohol-inspired compassion.

Gregory was just about to pull the door shut when Darryl called out to him, "This whole deal isn't your fault, is it?"

"Whatchoo talkin' about?"

"Your brother got you into this mess, didn't he?"

The most bloodcurdling psychopaths often have a compelling need to talk about themselves and how they've been judged unfairly, about how their disgusting actions are always someone else's fault. An unjust society, a rocky upbringing, et cetera. Darryl knew that and could sense that Gregory was standing at the door, wrestling with his desire to talk.

"Can't get into that," he said. "But yeah, this his deal. Was only a matter of time."

The door closed, the locks were slid back into place, and Gregory pounded back up the stairs and out of the building. The racket of his souped-up car seemed to hang suspended in the air long after he drove off.

"Why are you sucking up to that asshole?" Thelma snapped in a loud voice.

"I want to blow the back of his fucking head off even more than you do," Darryl shot right back. "But he doesn't need to know that, does he?" Thelma sighed.

"The last thing we need to be doing down here is fighting each other. Let's get free of this stuff so we can deal with him the next time he returns," Darryl said.

Gritting his teeth against the onslaught of splinters guaranteed to follow, Darryl started rolling across the floor toward Thelma, who also began her torturous journey toward him.

Under the floor, the rat could be heard scurrying about in the darkness, probably devouring the poison dropped off by Cousin Gregory. The smell of its decaying body would be horrendous in a few days.

But you're going to be long gone by the time that happens, right, Darryl?

CHAPTER 17

"Charlie! Where are you, sweetie?"

On the verge of drifting into badly needed slumber, Charles Hudson jerked back into full wakefulness. Now what?

"Gloria, what the hell are you talking about? I'm right beside you!" he replied crossly, turning so that his back was to his wife. Then he angrily grabbed his pillow and burrowed under it. Could he make his desire for sleep any more obvious?

"You know what I'm talking about, Charlie," Gloria said sweetly. "Your body's here, but your mind has been away ever since the announcement about Adrienne. Is everything okay?"

Charles Hudson sighed. Some people are able to sense when someone wants to be left alone, but unfortunately, Gloria couldn't. The two of them had been married for fifteen years and Hudson guessed she probably never would develop that knack.

Yanking the pillow from his face, Charles Hudson sat up in bed. "Gloria, unlike the work you do, being mayor of a major city is stressful as hell. I swim in an Olympic-sized pool of bullshit every damn day. Why is that so hard for you to understand?"

Hoping that would bring her queries to an end, Charles Hudson eased back down onto the bed, again turning his back to his wife.

"I know you, sweetie," she said quietly. "You treat me like I'm a moron sometimes, but I know you better than you think. Something is bothering you and I just thought you might want to talk about it. Is something going on between you and Gregory?"

Charles Hudson let loose a melodramatic sigh. He knew it was late and made a point of not glancing at the digital alarm clock. Sometimes it was better not to know how much sleep you were being deprived of. He sat up in bed again.

"No, nothing is happening between me and Gregory. Why?"

"Well, usually he never calls here. But ever since the news about Adrienne, he's called here about ten times. Even you'll admit that's kind of unusual, right?"

Charles Hudson reached over to the nightstand and snapped on the lamp. He looked over at Gloria, who shielded her face, not eager to be viewed without makeup. "To tell you the truth, Glo, I really hadn't noticed. I have a lot on my plate tomorrow, not to mention the damn press pestering me about Adrienne. Do you mind if I go to sleep now? Please?"

"Okay."

"Thanks."

This time it was Gloria Hudson who turned her back. Charles Hudson guessed her feelings were probably hurt, but if that's what it took to get a few hours of rest, so be it.

"I do have one more question," Gloria said in a tone that made it clear her husband needed to listen. "Are you still in love with Adrienne?"

Charles Hudson reached over to his wife and lightly rubbed her shoulder. "I am not in love with Adrienne," he said. "Fifteen years ago I hooked up with a beautiful woman that I am still happily married to. I would love her even more if she would let me go to sleep, though."

Gloria Hudson giggled. "Sweetie."

"Yeah, Glo."

"Did you know it's been two weeks since the last time we made love?"

Charles Hudson rolled his eyes. He'd had a couple of steamy liaisons with his mistress earlier in the day, and she had rocked his world both times.

Concentrate, Charles, concentrate.

He thought about some of the wild acts he and his mistress had engaged in, enabling him to achieve an erection for his wife. Then he had unenthusiastic sex with his Gloria, who moaned and shuddered as though being ravaged by the greatest swordsman on the planet.

She was dead-on in her assessment that something was bothering Charles Hudson. As much as he prided himself on his problem-solving skills, he was finally confronting something beyond his ability to tame.

He kept thinking about the safe house where Gregory had supposedly stashed the homicide detective and the reporter. Typical overkill on Gregory's part, and an overcorrection that would have to be dealt with.

Charles kept trying to imagine a scenario that would allow the hostages to emerge alive while he managed to remain in power. There had been more than enough senseless carnage already.

The more Charles Hudson focused on inaction, the more attractive that option became. Doing nothing would allow him to claim ignorance of the entire situation if it ever became public. Plus, if the status quo was maintained, the cop and the reporter would eventually die in the safe house, meaning they would no longer have to be dealt with.

That's what's been weighing on my mind, Gloria. If you must know.

DARRYL BILLUPS AND Thelma Holmes worked throughout the night at freeing themselves from what they called the Dungeon. Blood from Thelma's split nail now covered the knot that secured the plastic ropes around Darryl's wrists, making the plastic slippery.

But instead of getting frustrated, Thelma merely became more dogged in her quest to pry apart the bindings around Darryl's wrists. Sometime around 7:00 A.M., they finally appeared to loosen. Not a lot, but enough to give Thelma hope that she might be on the right track.

The sun was up now, as a bright yellow line was starting to appear under the wooden basement door.

"I think we're on to something here!" Darryl cried out suddenly, starting to feel more and more play in the plastic binding his wrists. Plus, feeling was slowly starting to return to his fingers! Straining to move his arms apart even more, Darryl applied greater pressure to the plastic rope and could feel his arms slowly inching apart.

Apparently the knot was gone, allowing the rope to slowly come undone when Darryl pushed against it. After ten minutes, he had two inches of play to work with. Thirty minutes later, Darryl was able to move his hands four inches apart.

"Thelma, grab the rope around my right wrist," Darryl said excitedly. "I'll see if I can wriggle my hand out of this stuff."

"Got it," Thelma responded. Darryl noticed that her voice sounded weaker than when they first entered their makeshift prison. He began to violently swivel his aching left shoulder in a bid to free his left arm.

Darryl went through the ungainly-looking exercise five times while Thelma pulled at the ropes encircling his right wrist. During the sixth attempt, Darryl suddenly felt no more pressure or tension on his left wrist—it was finally free.

"We did it, Thelma. We did it!" he cried out, bringing his right arm in front of him. As he had suspected, it had several loops of white plastic clothesline tied around it. Darryl hurriedly got them off, then undid his feet.

He stood up, legs shaky as a newborn colt's from a lack of exercise and because the clothesline had caused his feet to fall asleep. He took a few tottering steps over to the ceiling light and snapped it on. Never before had such a simple act felt so incredibly empowering.

With the dank, dirty room bathed in sixty watts of light, Darryl walked over to Thelma and quickly undid the plastic shackles encircling her wrists and ankles.

Then Darryl gently helped Thelma to her feet, and she rose on legs equally unsteady. They gave each other a long, hard hug, oblivious to their splinters and smelly, urine-stained clothing.

Thelma was weeping, too, Darryl could tell. Not audibly, but enough for him to feel her sides moving as tears of gratitude flowed.

"Probably a good idea to walk around a little bit to get the blood flow back," Thelma said, squatting suddenly as though suffering a dizzy spell.

Darryl was at her side instantly. "You okay?"

"I'm fine," came the proud reply. "Legs just a little weak, that's all."

"You have an ankle holster, right?" Darryl asked, praying for an affirmative response.

Thelma frowned, still squatting. "That was the first thing I checked when you freed me," she said in a flat voice. "The bastard took it. But . . ."

Thelma reached into her blouse and quickly withdrew a small cell phone from her cleavage. She clicked the wafer-thin silver phone on, punched in 911, and hit the send button.

Darryl was so elated that he gave Thelma a hard clap on the back, earning him an odd look and a grimace due to the splinters embedded in her back. But just as quickly as his hopes were raised, they were cruelly deflated: The thick cinder-block walls of their prison and the sturdy wooden door blocking their exit effectively blocked the microwaves Thelma's cell phone needed to operate.

"Let's move around the room and see if we can get the reception to improve," Darryl said hopefully.

They walked throughout the room, the little green light on the phone accompanying them as they did. They tried to dial 911 twenty times from various points in the room and even knelt near the small crack under the door, but the calls just wouldn't go through.

"Shit!" Darryl shouted. "How about Mace, Thelma? Do you have any Mace?"

She laughed weakly. "What in the world would a homicide cop need Mace for, Darryl? But I do have this."

She reached into an inner pocket of her jacket and pulled out the small brown purse she had walked into the Kit-Kat with. As Darryl watched raptly, Thelma snapped open the purse and pulled out a pair of silver police department handcuffs. Darryl smiled approvingly, instantly appreciating the significance of this last item.

"Got anything else in your bag of tricks?"

"That's it, I'm afraid."

Circulating around their basement holding cell with the cell phone gave them an appreciation of the degree to which their ordeal had fatigued and weakened them. Darryl and Thelma had been deprived of food, water, and exercise for two days. It was clear that whatever assault they mounted on Gregory would have to be a team effort.

Placing both hands against the wall, Darryl pushed against it to flex the muscles in his legs. He would need them in a couple of seconds. "Let's give the door a shot," Darryl muttered to no one in particular.

The door had at least two massive locks on it that Darryl and Thelma could see. Plus it was constructed of thick, indestructible-looking wood that would probably require a police battering ram to breach.

None of that was going to deter Darryl from taking a shot at kicking the door open. He stood about fifteen feet from the door, jogged toward it and kicked it with all his might. All that managed to do was generate a tremendous racket and send particles of dust flying into the air.

In the movies, the door would have flown off its hinges after one hard kick. But all Darryl had succeeded in doing was painfully jamming his right ankle, to his frustration and embarrassment. Four more vicious roundhouse kicks followed, leading to a sprained big toe and a ruined pair of work shoes.

Seeing that he was running the risk of seriously injuring himself, Darryl wisely opted to save his energy. He turned to look at Thelma, who appeared to be mulling an assault on the door of her own. "It's not worth it," he said. "Let's save it for Gregory."

"Okay."

Out of the corner of his eye, Darryl saw a tan figure hurtling toward the unyielding wooden door at a high rate of speed. He turned just in time to see Thelma plow into the door with both feet. She bounced off the door much as a fly might bounce off a windowpane, landing awkwardly.

Hhhhmmmpppph!

Thelma stood up and casually walked toward the far end of the room, then ran at full tilt toward the door again. Instead of using her feet, this time she lowered her right shoulder. Given that she was a big-boned woman, Thelma put a significant lick on the door. *Whhoooommp!* The noise from the collision reverberated through the house.

Predictably, the door won again. Thelma stumbled after the second impact, breaking her fall with her hands as Darryl watched, shaking his head in amazement. Did she really think she could knock the door down after he'd failed to?

Fairly calm up to that point, now Thelma was visibly angry as she straightened up and began to rub her right shoulder.

"Do you still smell gasoline?" Darryl asked out of the blue, more to draw attention from her inability to weaken the door than anything else.

"It's probably still around," Thelma said, slowly sitting down on the floor as she kept rubbing her shoulder in a clockwise motion. She stopped for a second to remove the handcuff key from her purse and drop it into her pants pocket. "We're probably just used to it." She thought about the .357 Magnum resting on the shelf in her bedroom closet. God, if only there were some kind of Uri Geller psychokinetic trick to make that powerful weapon materialize in her hands right now.

She knew she was capable of shooting another human

being in order to save her own life. But the act of pointing a gun at Gregory Hudson and pulling the trigger would be freighted with something a lot deeper than self-defense. Thelma was ashamed to admit it, but she would gladly cap Gregory Hudson for no other reason than old-fashioned revenge.

As if that weren't bad enough, she felt capable of leaving his bleeding body in this godforsaken house, then tossing a match into the place and never looking back.

It had only taken a few hours to turn a by-the-book cop with years of valorous experience into a revenge-seeking vigilante. False imprisonment, assault and battery, and repeated death threats have a way of doing that.

Darryl sat down, too, directly in front of Thelma. "While we're waiting for Shithead to return, can you please help me get some of these splinters out of my hide?"

"Sure," Thelma grunted, still disgusted over her inability to beat down the door.

Darryl unbuttoned his tattered, vomit-stained shirt and slowly eased it over his head, revealing arms that fairly rippled with well-detailed muscles, a chest broadened by regular workouts, and a six-pack of tightly grouped abdominal muscles.

Thelma stared at Darryl's body with unabashed admiration. She did it for several seconds, too. The experience they'd been through had pretty effectively whittled away any inhibitions that might be left between them. She felt as if she'd known Darryl her entire life, and he felt the same way about her.

"Nice bod," Thelma said simply. Not only were Darryl's pecs and abs easy on the eyes, but it was reassuring to know he might be able to hold his own in a physical confrontation.

"Thanks," Darryl replied, without a hint of shyness. "Do you know why I asked you to come to the Kit-Kat? Because I think you're cute," he said boldly, not waiting for a response.

Hell, they might be dead in a few hours, so he might as well say what was really on his mind.

Thelma threw back her head and laughed heartily after Darryl's last statement. "You have got to be kidding," she said, gesturing toward her soiled, tattered clothes. "I look like a bag woman, Darryl!"

He laughed easily. "Attractiveness isn't just about what your exterior is like," he said. "I usually have an intuitive sense of what people have up here," Darryl said, pointing to his head. "And here," he added, tapping his chest. "Plus, women with handcuffs just turn me on! Lawd have mercy."

They both chuckled, their minds momentarily off the impending arrival of Gregory. Kneeling behind Darryl, Thelma used what was left of her fingernails to painstakingly remove as many of the splinters impaling his bruised and bloodied back as she could.

Then she removed her blouse and Darryl returned the favor. The whole time he gazed at the smooth skin on Thelma's back and at her pink bra, Darryl quietly wondered if he was performing his last good deed in life.

When he was finished, Thelma put her blouse back on; then she and Darryl lay on the floor, pressing their backs against each other. Even though it was a hot August day outside, the basement dungeon holding Darryl and Thelma was cool.

Finally free of their bindings and aware they were about to try something that would call for every last ounce of their remaining energy, Darryl and Thelma quickly faded off to sleep.

THE ROAR OF AN approaching V-8 car engine awoke Darryl and Thelma with a start. "That's him," Darryl said tersely. He rose quickly and walked over to the wooden door, pressing his ear against a slight crack between the door and the doorsill.

At the same time, Thelma slipped her brown purse back into an inner pocket of her suit jacket and slid her cell phone back into its hiding place. There was nothing but blackness showing under the door—apparently they had slept beyond sunset.

"We need to wrap this clothesline loosely around our ankles to make it look as though we're still bound," Darryl said as the rumbling of the engine grew louder and louder. "Lay on the floor with your hands behind your back, as though they're still bound, too. Whoever Gregory comes closest to first attacks him."

"Let's roll," Thelma said, lying down and wrapping the plastic line around her ankles so that from the front it looked tightly drawn. Behind her legs, where Gregory wouldn't be able to see, Thelma made a loose pile with the slack in the clothesline.

Darryl's heart was racing to the point where it didn't seem to have individual beats. He reached up to switch off the ceiling light, then lay on the floor himself, wrapping the plastic clothesline around his ankles and putting his unbound hands behind his back.

Should they just bum-rush Gregory the moment he opened the door? The din of the pounding V-8 stopped right outside the building, and Darryl and Thelma soon heard a door opening upstairs.

"Darryl," Thelma hissed fiercely.

"Yeah."

"We can't play pitty-pat with this motherfucker. We need to take him *out*!"

"Preaching to the choir, girlfriend."

The cloddish footsteps were coming down the stairs as Darryl silently prayed for either success or a quick, relatively painless death.

A key was being inserted into the lock of the room now, and turned one full, agonizingly slow revolution. Then the dead bolt slid through its housing, the raspy noise so loud it seemed to rival that of a train uncoupling.

The massive silhouette filled the doorway, pausing momentarily before striding confidently into the room.

"Bad news, darlings!" the familiar menacing voice boomed out. "Hizzoner say yo' asses is here to stay. So"—Gregory paused to laugh—"guess that mean no food and water."

He reached up to switch on the light and seemed mildly surprised that Darryl and Thelma were both near the back wall now and were facing in his direction.

"Sorry, you two 'bout to get busy or somethin'?" That comment was followed by another laugh. Gregory was in a jovial mood tonight, clearly enjoying his deadly work. "Well, this my last visit, y'all. Bye."

"Wait!" Thelma cried out as Gregory turned on his heel, about to walk out the door. "Can't a sister get a dying wish?"

Gregory cocked his head, looking at Thelma suspiciously. "Hurry up, bitch; I ain't got all night."

"Can I please, please please have one last cigarette?" Thelma was crying now, and Darryl knew it was because she was genuinely terrified—terrified of the homicidal, primitive side of her personality Gregory put her in touch with.

"Goddamn!" Gregory said, patting his pants pockets impatiently. "What I look like, the Salvation Army up in here?" Then he turned to walk out of the door and out of Darryl's and Thelma's lives forever.

Gregory had taken maybe three steps before Darryl hit him in the back with such force that he was briefly knocked airborne and thrust forward about six feet before sprawling face-first onto the wooden floor. The element of surprise allowed Darryl to get off five hard punches to Gregory's one as they tussled on the floor.

Darryl fought like an enraged animal, wielding an unnatural strength borne of desperation. A molar flew through the air and danced crazily along the floor to the right of Gregory's head. Darryl wasn't sure who it belonged to, nor did he care. A silver pistol materialized from Gregory's waistband, and fortunately the handgun was in the strong hands of one Thelma Holmes, who crashed the weapon repeatedly against Gregory's head.

She tried frantically to pull the trigger, but the safety was still on. Pummeling the madman with one vicious blow after another, the two prisoners somehow managed to flip Gregory on his stomach, Darryl perched on Gregory's back and raining punch after punch against his head.

Like an enraged bull, the bigger man roared to his feet, carrying Darryl perilously aloft, near the rough-hewn wooden support beams in the ceiling. The mayor's younger brother then stumbled backward onto Thelma, who entangled his legs. The three combatants tumbled to the floor in a heap, Thelma on the bottom and screaming in agony.

She had just managed to free the safety on Gregory's silver 9mm handgun when it skittered across the wooden floor, somersaulting into the hole where the rat had hidden.

Bucking frantically and trying to free himself of Darryl's arm, which was wrapped around his neck and choking off his air supply, Gregory rolled off Thelma and viciously elbowed Darryl in the side to get the smaller man away from his windpipe.

That was just the opening Thelma needed. Leaping to her feet, she pulled her leg back like a soccer kicker and unleashed an explosive shot that caught Gregory on his left testicle.

He slumped toward the floor, allowing Darryl to also scamper up to his feet. Aiming for Gregory's head, Darryl uncorked a wicked roundhouse kick that caught Gregory on the point of his chin. His head jerked back violently and the sadistic psychopath crumpled to the floor, unconscious.

At some point, it was clear to both Darryl and Thelma that Gregory was incapacitated and couldn't endanger either of them, but they continued to beat him, fueled by anger and frustration and adrenaline.

Finally, too weary to hit Gregory any longer, they collapsed on the floor themselves.

"We need to cuff this clown and bind his feet," Thelma said huffing and puffing, her eyes rolling back into her head from the exertion. She wearily extracted her brown purse from her suit jacket and removed her handcuffs from her stylish handbag.

Putting one of her feet in the small of Gregory's back, Thelma roughly pulled his arms behind his back and cuffed his wrists together. She tightened the cuffs a couple of clicks for good measure, to the point where they pinched the skin on Gregory's wrists. "Who's the *bitch* now?" she said hotly.

Meanwhile, Darryl had begun to bind Gregory's feet with the same white plastic clothesline he'd used to shackle Darryl and Thelma. Darryl was finishing up the last of four knots securing Gregory's legs just as he began to come to.

"Man, what the fuck?" Gregory said in a winded voice as he squinted at the bare ceiling light. "My head hurts like a sumbitch."

"You think it hurts now?" Darryl shouted. He stopped adjusting the knot he was working on and coldcocked Gregory with a vicious right hand that bounced his head off the floor.

"Damn—brutality!" Thelma said with mock dismay. "That's police brutality, isn't it, Greg? Oh—damn, Darryl isn't a cop. That's right; I forgot! Guess that means he could kick your ass all night, huh?"

Gregory responded by spewing a mouthful of blood and saliva in Darryl's direction. "I ain't afraid of neither one a you muthafuckas," he said in a low, mean voice.

Thelma laughed lightly. "Lemme tell you something," she said, holding her bloody fingernails up to the light and examining them closely. Then she looked Gregory directly in the eye.

"If Darryl wasn't here, I'd kill you right now," Thelma said, sneering. "And I'd do it slowly, so I could enjoy it. And I'd swear that it was self-defense.

"But luckily for you, shithead—" Thelma suddenly leapt at Gregory Hudson, catching him with a long, looping left hand that smacked against his forehead. "Luckily for you, Darryl *is* here."

Darryl hadn't realized Thelma was left-handed until that moment.

"Forget him—let's go get some water," Darryl said.

Bounding up a set of narrow, wooden steps, Darryl and Thelma flew through the darkened upstairs of the dwelling. They could see a streetlight. And it was shining through the upstairs windows of their prison, as well as through a door that had two glass windowpanes.

Both former captives bumped into the door in their haste to exit the building that had imprisoned them for two days. The doorway led to a narrow street bounded on both sides by heavy woods. Darryl and Thelma sprinted across the street into the woods and immediately found themselves stumbling and falling through thick underbrush and leaves.

Tree branches and spiderwebs struck Darryl in the face as he continued to run, fearful of stopping until the streetlight had receded to a little point of light barely visible through the tree branches.

Neither he nor Thelma knew where they were, nor did they particularly give a damn—it just felt good to breathe in pure air. They were both sailing, ecstatic to be out of the hell-hole that had held them for a two-day eternity. Darryl was able to appreciate the profound relief runaway slaves must have felt after finally seizing a liberty that should have been their birthright.

He and Thelma dropped to their bellies in the under-brush, not daring to make a sound in case someone had followed them. But they didn't hear a thing, except for the sound of crickets and the insistent cry of a whippoorwill.

When it was clear that they weren't being pursued, Darryl did what came naturally—he turned to Thelma and kissed her. But instead of a relieved peck on her cheek or forehead, he kissed her full on the lips. She returned his kiss, to Darryl's surprise, without turning her head or flinching.

"We need to figure out where we are," Darryl said, still peering in the direction of the streetlight, finding it hard to believe no one was chasing them.

"I'm gonna call Donatelli," Thelma said, already back into cop mode. "Why don't you head back toward the street and see if you can spot a street sign or something?"

Moving back toward the street on his belly, like a combat soldier advancing under hostile fire, Darryl went to reconnoi-ter their position. If he stayed prone, that would make him extremely hard to spot. Darryl wasn't going back into that basement—he would die first.

After moving forward a few yards, Darryl was surprised to discover that he and Thelma were in the backyard of a nineteenth-century house set back from the road. No lights were on in the wooden dwelling, which was painted red, nor

were there any vehicles in the driveway. Only after deter-
mining that did Darryl resume his forward motion.

When he was almost to the street, he could see the house
they'd managed to escape. It also featured nineteenth-century
architecture, was made of brick, and decorated with white
paint and black shutters. A late-model blue Ford Mustang was
parked to the side of the house.

Crouching now, Darryl saw an old-fashioned black-and-
white street sign that said: WETHERDSVILLE ROAD. Then he
scampered back up the slight incline to Thelma's position. On
the way back, he noticed the empty red house appeared to
have an outdoor faucet for a garden hose.

"We're on Wetherdsville Road," he whispered after safely
making it back to Thelma's side. "Near a white house with a
blue Mustang beside it."

"Did you hear that, Scott?" she said in a low voice. "We're
located somewhere on Wetherdsville Road, near a white
house with a blue Mustang near it . . . Okay. We'll hang tight
until then."

She looked at Darryl and smiled. "He's on his way."

They remained on their bellies for five minutes, then ten
minutes, then twenty minutes, and Donatelli still hadn't
arrived.

"I am dying of thirst," Darryl whispered.

"Me, too."

"We're not too far from a house with a faucet. It's been
two days since we've had any water. We should be safe up
here."

Without exchanging another word, they began to slink
toward the house Darryl had seen, with him leading the way.

The outdoor faucet obviously hadn't been turned on for a
while, judging from the huge air bubbles that burbled out
when Darryl turned it on. Cupping his hands together, he

greedily ladled water into his mouth, drinking until he was out of breath. Then he stood watch while Thelma drank.

At one point they both stuck their heads under the faucet and indulged in the luxury of rinsing dirt and grime out of their hair.

But they both stopped and turned off the water after spotting the approaching headlights of a distant car. Much quieter than Gregory's hot-rod Mustang, it glided in front of the white house with black shutters and killed its engine. Darryl and Thelma could see that it was a white, unmarked city police vehicle.

Still, they approached the vehicle carefully, until seeing Donatelli's long black hair through the passenger window. He was already out of his vehicle, chomping on his toothpick and smiling by the time Darryl bounded toward him.

"Scott!"

"You okay, man?"

"Man, you wouldn't believe what's been going on here. God, man, you just wouldn't believe it. We found the murderer."

"To tell you the truth, I'm not surprised," Donatelli said, running a hand through his long hair. He looked tremendously relieved. "My partner is a helluva detective." He walked over and gave Darryl a big hug. "Is Detective Holmes okay? Detective Holmes!"

Thelma ran out of the woods next, her hair soaking wet, and looked at Donatelli with a shocked expression. Without saying a word, he immediately gave her a hug, too—a little longer than was necessary for a platonic professional relationship, it seemed to Darryl.

"The dirtbag who hired Alonzo Ellis is downstairs in the basement," Thelma said proudly, pointing toward the open front door of the white house.

"I'll call for backup," Donatelli said, heading for the door.

"No need," Thelma said, suddenly stiff and professional. "He's cuffed—all we need to do is Miranda him."

"I'll be a son of a bitch," Donatelli said. "Lemme see this turd who got me shot."

The three of them headed into the house and flicked on a light. They briefly checked out the first floor, which was without furniture except for a wooden kitchen table and two chairs. Then they headed toward the basement, with Darryl eagerly envisioning a three-way tag team beatdown of Gregory Hudson.

Imperturbable when up against Darryl and Thelma, Gregory Hudson looked like he saw a ghost as soon as Donatelli entered the room.

"So, this is the man who got me capped?" Donatelli said calmly. " 'Fraid I have to be the bearer of bad tidings, big guy," he added, pulling out a Beretta Cougar .32-caliber semi-automatic pistol. Thelma immediately recognized that the weapon wasn't Donatelli's service revolver.

"Unfortunately, the boss says nobody gets to leave, including you," Donatelli said blandly.

Gregory Hudson's eyes widened, but he never uttered a word of protest as Donatelli placed the muzzle of the Beretta against Hudson's left ear and pulled the trigger once. The sound of the fatal shot was no louder than a cap pistol, because the bulk of the explosion had been muffled by the left hemisphere of Hudson's brain.

Darryl and Thelma looked at Donatelli, mouths agape.

"That's the way it goes sometimes," Donatelli said, casually wiping the muzzle of the Beretta on Gregory Hudson's shirt. "You guys did a fantastic job tracking down this cretin," he continued, turning to Darryl and Thelma with his pistol still in his hand. "Too bad no one will ever find out."

Donatelli pointed the weapon at Darryl, who was reaching inside the jacket he'd borrowed from Mad Dawg. "Come on now, Darryl. Put your hands where I can see them, bro'."

Darryl slowly pulled out his hand, which held a stick of chewing gum, and raised it over his head.

"Scott . . . you've lost your mind, right?" Thelma said in utter disbelief. "What in God's name are you doing?"

Maybe it was Darryl's imagination, but Donatelli actually appeared to be embarrassed. "An old story, Thelma—do you mind if I call you that?" he asked facetiously. Donatelli waved his gun toward the floor. "Why don't you guys go ahead and lie down while I tell you a bedtime story?"

Darryl and Thelma slowly, grudgingly, got to their knees and stretched out once again on the splinter-filled wood floor they had become all too familiar with over the last forty-eight hours. Moving deliberately, Darryl took off Mad Dawg's jacket, folded it, and laid it on the floor.

"I like a man who takes good care of his clothes," Donatelli said, twirling his toothpick between his lips.

"Belongs to a friend," Darryl said. "I would hate to get blood on it," he added sarcastically.

"Whatever you've gotten yourself into, Scott," Thelma said slowly, "maybe we can still figure a way out of it. It's not too late."

Donatelli smiled warmly, then clapped his hands twice, taking care to maintain his grip on his weapon. "Bravo, bravo, Thelma," he said. "A most convincing performance. You know as well as I do that you'd have Internal Affairs up my ass two seconds after we left this place.

"Anyway," he continued, "it's a little late in the game for me to turn back now."

"What's going on, Scott?" Thelma said again slowly, still not fully comprehending.

Reaching behind him, Donatelli tapped his wallet twice with the Beretta. "What's going on, Thelma," he said soberly, "is two hundred and fifty thousand dollars. Courtesy of our illustrious commander in chief, Mayor Charles Hudson."

Donatelli paused, awaiting Darryl's and Thelma's reactions. Their lack of response disappointed him.

"Come on, folks," he said with mock disappointment. "We may be living in the twenty-first century, but that's still an awful lot of money. Especially," Donatelli added with a wink, "if it's been wired to an offshore account in the Bahamas that Uncle Sammy can't put his grimy little hands on."

"Lemme guess," Darryl spoke up. "Hudson is giving you this as a bonus for being such a good detective, right?"

"Actually, you're partially right, Darryl. I managed to find out that the mayor and his little brother here were both poking Adrienne Hudson back when she was engaged to the mayor."

Donatelli paused and jabbed at Gregory Hudson with his foot. He kicked Hudson gently several times, until he heard a jingling noise. Stooping down and keeping his Beretta pointed in the general direction of Darryl and Thelma, Donatelli reached into Gregory Hudson's right pocket and pulled out a set of keys.

"Can't have Greg's hot-rod Mustang sitting around out front," Donatelli said. "That would only draw suspicion." He nodded toward the basement door. "And I can't leave that door unlocked, because one of you might leave Pandora's box and spill all my little secrets. Right, Darryl?"

Darryl said nothing, wondering what would happen if he or Thelma tried to rush Donatelli. Would the detective fire and miss wildly, surprised by the sudden movement? Or would it be a simple matter to pump a bullet into the top of one of their heads?

Donatelli gestured toward Gregory Hudson. "Anyway, lover boy here kills Adrienne Hudson in a fit of jealous rage, figuring that if he can't have her, nobody can. The mayor saw it all and hasn't said jack all these years."

Donatelli gave a bitter little laugh. "Voters can stomach a lot of faults in politicians, but they kind of draw the line when it comes to being an accessory to murder."

"So you and Gregory have been working together?" Darryl asked, hands behind his head, fingers interlocked.

"I've known Gregory longer than I've known you," Donatelli said. "He was basically a two-bit hood that judges always slapped on the wrist because of his brother." Looking down at Gregory Hudson, Donatelli's lips turned down disapprovingly. "He was a rank amateur."

As Thelma listened to Donatelli, the features of her pretty face twisted into a furious scowl. "You piece of shit!" she screamed. "That's why you had a bullet-proof vest on at the Safe&Sound. We never wear those things, but you *knew* we were going to be fired on!"

Donatelli shrugged. "Greg was in way over his head with this one," he said easily, as though making small talk about the weather. "He was three storage units down from where you shot that kid. Do you think that Alonzo Ellis killed two people with some peashooter .22-caliber? That was our boy Greg here. And he was supposed to take you out, too."

Grimacing, the long-haired homicide detective paused to rub his damaged rib. "He definitely wasn't supposed to shoot me, even though I had a vest on. I think Greg's MENSA membership lapsed."

Darryl looked puzzled and Donatelli noted it. "Spit it out, Darryl—you reporters are always full of questions. Might as well ask, because I don't think we'll be seeing your byline in the *Herald* anymore."

Raising his head so that he could look at Donatelli straight on, Darryl took his shot. "Does the mayor actually know we're here?" he asked incredulously.

"Yep."

"And he sent you here to kill his own brother!"

Donatelli smiled, amused at Darryl's naïveté. "If I were your brother, Darryl . . . and I was boning your fiancée on a regular basis, then *killed her,* would you feel warm and fuzzy about me?" Shaking his head, Donatelli enjoyed a laugh at Darryl's expense.

A brother killing a brother over a woman was old hat. Elected officials feel the same passions, confront the same demons, as anyone else.

"We're not getting out of here, are we, Scott?" Thelma asked bluntly.

Donatelli stopped smiling and exhaled slowly. He clearly wasn't taking any satisfaction out of what he had to do. "No, Thelma. The mayor doesn't think it would be a great idea for the two of you to be running around."

It grew eerily quiet in the room. A few seconds earlier, Darryl and Thelma had been over the moon, ecstatic over their escape. Now the horrible realization that they would never be leaving was settling in.

Darryl smiled grimly, remembering that he had promised himself he would depart this room. And for a few fantastic, freedom-filled moments, he had. *I should have promised myself that I would live to see another day!*

"If I were to let you guys go," Donatelli said hopefully, "do you think you could avoid our friends in Internal Affairs?"

Darryl turned to stare at his coprisoner. For several agonizing moments she said nothing. Then she nodded, with a head movement so subtle that it could barely be seen.

"That a yes, Thelma?"

She nodded again, refusing to look up at her former partner. Darryl couldn't believe Thelma was being a straight arrow at a moment like this. Integrity had its place, but so did living.

"You need to give that some more thought," Darryl said heatedly.

Thelma looked up this time and spoke in a weary-sounding voice. "Darryl, when you get in bed with a snake, it's going to strike eventually. Scott is a snake, his word isn't worth shit, and you can bet he's got a couple of bullets with our names on them. Regardless of what I say."

Looking as though it pained and disgusted her to do so, Thelma glanced up at Donatelli. "I'm just curious about one thing, Scott. How did you get mixed up in this?"

Incredibly, Donatelli appeared to be upset about having been characterized as a "snake" by his partner. His shoulders had slumped noticeably and his lips were clamped forlornly around his toothpick.

"Gregory had a way of getting very giddy and talkative when he got drunk," Donatelli said curtly. "I went to this dive bar he owns one night when he was sloshed out of his mind. He talked about a little problem he and his brother were having. So, I approached the mayor and offered my services."

"You mean you blackmailed the mayor," Darryl shot back, still furious at Thelma for refusing to humor Donatelli.

"No, Darryl, I never threatened the mayor. Things just sort of worked out. Not only did I get a quarter mil out of this deal, but in a few weeks Tuck Anders is going to be shoved aside as the homicide lieutenant. Guess who's about to get promoted?"

"Congratulations," Thelma spit out sarcastically. "Nothing beats a meritocracy, does it?" She motioned toward Gregory's lifeless body. "And thanks for telling caveman over there that me and Darryl were coming to the Kit-Kat."

"Don't mention it, Thelma. Now if we're finished talking here"—Donatelli raised the Beretta and pointed it at Thelma— "let's go ahead and get this over with."

Thelma Holmes never flinched, nor did Darryl expect her to. Donatelli unexpectedly lowered his gun and looked at Darryl. "You know, Darryl, you're a clever one," he said. "But if you have one drawback, it's that you can be kind of predictable sometimes. You can go ahead and take it out now."

"What are you talking about?"

Donatelli's eyes narrowed. "Don't play with me, Darryl. I know it's in the breast pocket of your jacket. I can *hear* the damn thing, for chrissakes! Hand it over. And do it slowly, unless you want to get shot first."

Darryl eased his right hand into the breast pocket of Mad Dawg's jacket. He fumbled a bit before extracting a microcassette recorder that had a small red light on it, indicating the unit was recording. Darryl looked at Donatelli defiantly.

"You gonna slide it over to me, or do you want me to come get it, Darryl? Take your pick."

Darryl shoved the tape recorder across the floor with such force that it scooted past Donatelli and smacked against the far wall. Keeping an eye on his captives, Donatelli calmly fetched the machine and pushed a button, ejecting the cassette onto the floor. Donatelli then took his right shoe and ground the cassette under his heel, shattering it with a loud crunching noise.

"Cute, Darryl," Donatelli said, twirling his toothpick between his teeth. He hurled the microcassette recorder against the cinder-block wall, and the electronic device exploded into bits of shrapnel that ricocheted throughout the small room.

One of the double A batteries twirled and pirouetted toward Darryl, hitting him in the hand.

Looking remorseful, Donatelli raised his Beretta again, drawing a bead on Thelma's head.

"You're first," he said grimly, squinting his right eye in preparation to fire.

"Scott, let me show you something," Thelma said in a quiet, determined voice. Pushing herself up, she rose to her knees and slowly opened her blouse. Her hand dipped into her ample cleavage as Donatelli squinted at Thelma over the barrel of his pistol, ready to blow her away if she as much as hiccuped.

Thelma pulled out the little silver cell phone and flipped it open. "When I was outside, I didn't call for backup because Darryl and I didn't need it," Thelma said slowly. "But I did call the crime lab and I did call Lieutenant Anders to let him know that we were here and that we were all right." Spoken with a tone at once triumphant and condescending.

The test of wills and one-upmanship that characterized their relationship would last to the very end, and she had won the final round, Thelma seemed to be saying with her words and the smirk on her face.

"They're probably on their way right now—I contacted them about fifteen minutes before you walked through the door."

Donatelli gave a snorting laugh—partially because he admired Thelma's moxie and partially because she was wasting her last breath on an obvious whopper.

"If you don't believe me," she said, shrugging, "push the redial button on my phone and see what number comes up. You blew it *big-time*, Scott."

Thelma casually tossed the phone across the room to Donatelli's right, the same side as his gun, making him take three small steps to catch the phone with his left hand before it hit the ground. In the time it took him to perform that act, Darryl brushed aside Mad Dawg's sport coat, revealing the rat hole in the floor.

Darryl thrust his hand into the hole, felt something hard and cold, and yanked it out with a brutal motion. He hit his hand on one of the wooden floor slats but maintained his grip on Gregory's gun. Several shots rang out in rapid succession—Darryl couldn't tell if they were from his weapon or Donatelli's.

A bullet shattered the bare lightbulb hanging from the ceiling, plunging the room into partial darkness. Darryl frantically squeezed the trigger of Gregory's handgun over and over and over, until finally it stopped firing.

Realizing that he was out of ammunition, Darryl froze on the floor, afraid to move, afraid to even breathe. He held his breath, watching dreamlike clouds of grayish-blue gun smoke drift through the light streaming through the open door.

Goddammit, somebody say something.

Darryl heard a loud *clunk!* from the area of the room where Donatelli had been. It was the sound of something heavy and metallic hitting the floor, followed by the musical jangling of spent handgun shells raining to the ground.

"You okay, Darryl?" Thelma asked in a strained voice. It seemed to be coming from the area where Donatelli had been standing.

"I think so."

"Well, help me find my cell phone!" she snapped.

Darryl was instantly high as a kite as an indescribable euphoria flooded through him. Nor did his high leave him when a low, guttural moan filled the room, a room that had almost become Darryl's final resting place. That moan was Scott Donatelli's.

Tossing aside Gregory's now useless weapon, Darryl groped his way toward Thelma's voice and literally stumbled over Donatelli's body.

"I've got his service revolver and his other piece," Thelma said. "Drag him outside into the light, and I'll call for backup once I find my phone."

Darryl put his arms under Donatelli's and pulled the wounded detective out of the Dungeon and into the next room. He was barely conscious and bleeding heavily from a wound near his right collarbone, as well as a gunshot wound to his left hand and left buttocks.

Hyperventilating and shaking like a leaf in a hurricane, Darryl sat down on the narrow stairwell and gazed in shock at Donatelli, who was slowly shaking his head back and forth.

Thelma came barreling out of the room and nearly knocked Darryl off the stairs as she wordlessly raced upstairs and out of the house.

Even though Donatelli had been ready to end Darryl's life a few seconds earlier, Darryl didn't want the detective to die. Spiritual but hardly religious, Darryl rose from the steps and knelt over Donatelli's bleeding body.

Darryl surprised himself with a gesture he hadn't performed since he was a teenager—he made the sign of the cross. Then he prayed for Donatelli's life and for the salvation of Gregory's soul.

Having done that, Darryl turned and ran up the stairs, scooting out of the house and into the humid night air. He turned to look with new eyes at the nineteenth-century dwelling he'd just exited, the woods surrounding it—even the moths flitting around the street lamp.

Spotting Donatelli's police vehicle, Darryl jogged toward it. Thelma was sitting in the driver's seat, using the police radio. As Darryl clambered into the passenger seat, he and

Thelma exchanged glances, but never said a word. As power-ful as the English language is, there are times when it's just an assemblage of meaningless utterances.

So Darryl and Thelma said what needed to be said with another long hug, then silently awaited the arrival of police officers and fire department paramedics.

EPILOGUE

Scott Donatelli survived the gunshot injuries sustained in an empty rental house in Dickeyville, an all-white enclave in Northwest Baltimore that has been designated a national historic site. The community consists of 134 homes that are located in a heavily wooded area and preserved to look as they did in the nineteenth century.

Dickeyville is the last place police would have searched for Darryl Billups and Thelma Holmes had they been unable to elude their captors.

Donatelli lost such a large percentage of his right lung that a resumption of his police career was out of the question. Not that his physical disability would have mattered—he was fired from the police department and convicted of first-degree murder in the shooting death of Gregory Hudson.

Donatelli was sentenced to twenty-five years without

parole in the Jessup Correctional Facility, a massive state prison complex south of Baltimore. The detective's street smarts allowed him to fit in easily with Jessup's majority African-American population.

Police technicians easily recovered the contents of the microcassette Donatelli had damaged. The cassette's evidentiary value was strong enough for a grand jury to indict Baltimore mayor Charles Hudson on counts of obstruction of justice, bribery, and solicitation of murder.

Hudson was forced to resign from office and had to assume a second mortgage on his unattractive brown-and-white Tudor to cover the cost of his legal fees. He hired one of the nation's best-known black defense attorneys, who spectacularly justified his exorbitant fee.

But even the high-priced mouthpiece couldn't prevent the court from forcing Hudson to submit to a DNA test to determine the paternity of the fetus removed from Adrienne Jackson's body. Tissue samples were also taken from Gregory Hudson's body for testing. To Hudson's chagrin, DNA technicians determined that Gregory Hudson had fathered the baby growing inside Adrienne Hudson's womb at the time of her death.

At the end of the trial, avidly followed around the country, Charles Hudson was acquitted of all the charges filed against him. Afterward, he moved from Baltimore to Maryland's bucolic Eastern Shore, where he briefly practiced real estate law. He was subsequently brought up on charges related to the disappearance of Adrienne Jackson's body from the medical examiner's office in Baltimore.

The city's health commissioner had had severe misgivings about his role in helping to spring Jackson's body and confessed to state authorities several months later. He implicated Hudson, who was found guilty of violating Maryland laws related to the operation of the state medical examiner's office.

In addition to being disbarred and fined $25,000, Hudson received a three-year sentence in the Eastern Shore Correctional Facility. Not long after he began serving his sentence, Gloria Hudson delivered her husband a taste of his own medicine by engaging in a highly public affair with a fitness trainer from a nearby health spa.

Insisting on returning to work the next day after his escape from Dickeyville, Darryl Billups wrote a spectacular series of *Baltimore Herald* articles chronicling his and Thelma Holmes's experience as captives, not to mention their brush with death.

When his series was finished, Darryl put in for a vacation day, keeping a promise he'd made to himself before his improbable escape from Dickeyville. Darryl had a very important trip planned, and he'd need at least one bag full of chicken necks to fully enjoy himself.